HEAR NO EVIL

Dead and Buried

HEAR NO EVIL

HEAR NO EVIL

Dead and Buried

Kate Chester

SCHOLASTIC INC.
New York Toronto London Auckland Sydney

ISBN 0-590-67329-7

Copyright © 1996 by Leslie Davis Guccione.
All rights reserved. Published by Scholastic Inc.
HEAR NO EVIL is a trademark of Scholastic Inc.

12 11 10 9 8 7 6 5 4 3 2 1   6 7 8 9/9 0 1/0

Printed in the U.S.A.   01

First Scholastic printing, December 1996

To the Reader:

Sara Howell is profoundly, postlingually deaf (meaning she lost her hearing after she learned to speak). She is fluent in American Sign Language (ASL), and English. She can read lips.

When a character speaks, quotation marks are used: "Watch out for that bus!" When a character signs, *italics* are used to indicate ASL: *Watch out for that bus!* Quotation marks and *italics* indicate the character is signing and speaking simultaneously: *"Watch out for that bus!"*

Unless the sign is described (for example: Sara circled her heart. *I'm sorry . . .*), the italicized words are translations of ASL into English, not literal descriptions of the grammatical structure of American Sign Language.

Chapter 1

Sara Howell glanced at her watch. Ten minutes till the end of her break. Even counting the return through the labyrinth of basement hallways to the museum conference rooms, she had plenty of time. HALL OF ARCHITECTURE: a small arrow pointed up a narrow staircase. No sign said EMPLOYEES ONLY or NO ADMITTANCE so she grabbed the railing and ran up the steps two at a time. She caught her breath as she reached the top. She was at the back of a huge marble foyer, surrounded by towering examples of ancient architecture.

A bronze cat served as the newel post on the top of the banister. The reproduction of an incarnated Egyptian deity sat upright.

Sara followed the cat's gaze. It stared straight ahead to a wall mural of the Nile Valley.

On either side of the mural two reproductions of Sphinxes framed the entrance to the Egyptian Room. Two men stood at the base of the Sphinx, deep in conversation. A photo identification tag dangled from the chest pocket of the taller one. Sara read their body language instinctively. The tall balding official gestured toward the Egyptian Room. The shorter man pulled a piece of paper from his blazer pocket and nodded.

Pointing fingers, sweeping gestures, agreeable nods. It didn't take much to figure out that they were discussing some aspect of the coming Eldridge exhibit, maybe the layout for the priceless artifacts, or high-powered security for the Saturday night gala that preceded the Sunday opening.

Out of all the high school students who had taken courses at the museum, Sara Howell and Keesha Fletcher, both from Radley Academy, had been asked to participate in what promised to be the social event of the holiday season. Art lovers, society matrons, and business elite from all over Radley were paying a thousand dollars a plate to attend a preview of the Eldridge Collection and meet the millionaire art collector. R.C. Eldridge was said to have amassed a priceless collection associated with the ancient world: authentic relics from Egypt and Greece as well as reproductions that had belonged to eighteenth- and nineteenth-century European royalty.

For a thousand dollars patrons could attend the Saturday night gala, support the museum's art education program, and hobnob with Eldridge himself. Keesha was to work in the Egyptian Room. Sara in the Greek Room.

Lights were on in the room. Still, the space felt cold and foreboding. Two storage carts of folded circular tables sat in the middle of the room. Gilt chairs were piled three deep in front of plaster casts of Greek and Roman statues.

Behind her skinny saints lined up over massive doors of a Gothic cathedral front. Gargoyles grinned down at her. She craned her neck and squinted up at the dark rectangles of skylights three stories overhead. Her shoulder-length hair swung slightly. Not even dust motes moved in the track lighting.

She ran across the marble floor trying to shake the feeling that something was wrong. It wasn't until she was half inside a Greek temple entrance that it came to her. She spun back around. There was no sign of the two men. She was alone.

It was barely four o'clock. The museum was open for another hour but there was no sign of life anywhere in the hall. Downstairs the conference room was crowded with the socially prominent volunteers who were going over last minute details for the museum's glittering holiday party. Despite the snow falling outside, she was sure other exhibit rooms were busy. The parking lot had been full when she and Keesha had arrived.

None of that mattered. The Hall of Architecture was deserted. She walked further into the Greek Room. Empty cases where the Eldridge Collection would be displayed were set up in front of the Greek edifices. A moment of fear stopped her in her tracks.

She was framed on either side by fluted, granite columns that rose twenty feet over her head. The alarm system. During the break in the meeting downstairs she hadn't told anyone she was coming up here. What if someone in the meeting had announced that the hall was off limits? She wouldn't have heard; couldn't have heard. The guard had given no indication that he'd seen her. She looked up at the tiny electric eye cameras that scanned the museum, then over to the Grand Staircase which ran down to the street entrance. She could just make out the lobby. It was blocked by gates that had been pulled across the stairs.

Her heart sank then rose to her throat. On the other side of the gates, it was dark. The reception desk was empty. She could see past the darkened gift shop and through the glass doors. Snow drifted outside. Shut; locked; closed for the exhibit. No receptionist; no guides.

She knocked her forehead with her fist, American Sign Language for *stupid*. Why hadn't she realized . . . the security system! She turned frantically for some indication of whether she'd set off some ear-splitting setup of bells and sirens. The columns continued in front of her. They were huge, wide enough to hide behind. Her first, childish instinct was to press herself behind one like some cat burglar from an old movie. She didn't dare take another step forward. Even if she hadn't set off the alarm, she still could . . . and not hear it. She pivoted slowly, careful not to touch the columns, or anything else connected with the exhibit.

The Sphinxes stared. The gargoyles grinned. She could feel the vacant stare of the banister cat in the middle of her back. There was no vibration in the floor. No guards were leaping at her from the staircase. Still, for all she knew the alarm was blasting from every corner of the building. Worse, maybe she'd tripped a secret alarm that rang in some distant section of the museum to alert the authorities.

The hearing world had all kinds of sounds she couldn't remember. She pressed her hand to her ribs to slow her heart and get it from her throat back into her chest.

Her twenty-two-year-old brother, Detective Stephen Howell, loved to explain sophisticated protection systems: motion detectors, closed-circuit televisions, laser beams, sound waves. She shook her hands as if she could shake off the beams she imagined were bouncing off her. Maybe the museum was wired directly to the police station. She glanced up at the gargoyles, unable to decipher which made her heart race faster, the fear that she had set off an alarm, or the fear that Steve would answer the call if she had and be furious.

Sara started back down the narrow back staircase. A shadow broke her stride. It lengthened across the bottom steps. She stopped. A figure appeared from around the bend in the corridor. He was dressed in a uniform and his mouth was set in a grim line, his eyebrows puckered in concentration. He shoved his right hand to his hip. Sara cringed against the wall and winced, expecting to look down the barrel of a service revolver.

Chapter 2

Instead the guard palmed a cellular phone and spoke into it.

"No. Don't call anyone," she called out. "I'm coming from the meeting for Saturday's party. I got lost." She hurried down the stairs to him and prayed he had understood her muffled speech. She tapped her ear for good measure. "I'm deaf. I'm sorry. Did I set off the alarm?"

The security guard seemed to be breathing quickly as his face relaxed. "You damn well did. You scared the living daylights out of me. You tripped the whole system. Lucky for you they've got you under surveillance from the security room. Who gave you permission . . ."

She tapped her ear again. Until the death of her father in August, she'd spent most of the year in a residential school for the deaf, an entire community where ASL was the primary language. Even with practice, she only understood about fifty percent of any stranger's speech. This time had been easy. The guard's arched eyebrow, and wagging finger told her much of what she needed to know.

"I'm sorry," she repeated. "I thought it would be all right. Another guard was up there."

"What guard?"

She shrugged as she came down the rest of the stairs. "He has identification on his pocket." She held up two fingers. "Two men."

The guard looked skeptical. "We closed the room at three because of the exhibit. No one else had clearance to be up there and no one else set off the system." He yanked his thumb toward the bottom of the stairs in a gesture that said clearly: Don't give me excuses, just get going.

Sara glanced at the T. Maloney printed on his plastic nameplate. "Thanks. I'm sorry."

He shook his head. "In the camera room, security saw who you were and sent me after you. Stay where you belong!" He gave her a final distracted nod as Sara hurried back to the meeting where she belonged.

She did belong. Even Steve had asked her to stop dwelling on why, of all the students who took museum art classes, she'd been picked to represent the program the night of the preview fund-raiser.

"Two minicourses," she'd said to him the night before, holding up two fingers. "I took two weeks of pottery over winter break last year and eight classes in jewelry making before I left for camp last summer. I wasn't even very good."

Steve met her glance. He had a way of getting right into her brain, even when he struggled to understand her speech. He tapped his ears. "You think they want to show you off because you're deaf? Looks good if they have a deaf kid? Raises more money?" He jabbed his thumb toward the wall that separated their Thurston Court apartment from the Fletchers'. "You probably think they just asked Keesha because she's African-American."

"Keesha takes classes all the time." *All the time,* she added in sign.

Steve had just smiled. "Then maybe they asked the two of you because you're both poised, attractive, and talented. Maybe you and Keesha are what the museum wants in its high school art students. Maybe they want to show you off no matter what color you are or whether your ears work or not."

Sara thought about the conversation as she ran back along the winding corridor. Steve saw right into the heart of everything. It was the way their father had been. It was part of what made her brother so good at figuring out people. It was what she hoped she'd inherited, too.

The twenty-two year old detective was Sara's legal guardian. After the death of their mother six years ago, home and haven for Sara had been the Edgewood School for the Deaf. Her sheltered deaf community was halfway across the country, safe from the unstructured, high-risk life of her father, Radley police lieutenant Paul Howell. That was the way he'd wanted it, but it elevated Steve to the intriguing older brother she saw only on vacations.

Steve was busy with his own life, in and out of hers mostly as chauffeur, advisor, role model. All that changed on a hot night at the end of August.

Orphan. She still hated the word. In the four months since her father had been killed, the worst of her grief had been replaced by stabs of guilt. Steve agreed that she belonged back in Radley now, but overnight her hard working, blond, blue-eyed brother had become parent, chaperon, interpreter. He hadn't had practice at any of it.

All they had was each other — and the state Department of Social Services. Sara was sixteen, which meant that for the next two years social workers would monitor every aspect of her life and Steve's, as well. His parenting skills, his social life, even her academic standing at Radley Academy were suddenly their business, too. There were days when Steve would have shipped her back to

Edgewood without a farewell, and days when she would gladly have packed herself. He didn't however, and neither did she. In their hearts they knew Sara was where she belonged.

Now she stopped at the intersection of two corridors. This was not the time to contemplate her personal life. To find her way back, she had to pay attention. The museum complex was a full city block in length and Radley's cultural center was connected by a maze of hallways that snaked along the basement in every possible direction. She passed classrooms, storage halls, studios, and management offices. Down here is a world unto itself, she thought.

She used up more than the ten minutes allotted for the break. Embarrassment replaced her fear as she returned to the conference room. Geneva Johnson, the museum director for special events, was at the head of the room. She stopped talking until Sara had returned to her place next to Keesha.

As the adults involved in the fund-raiser turned to stare at her, Keesha smiled sympathetically. *She explained what happened,* Keesha signed. *I should have told you that when she gave us the break, she announced not to go upstairs. I thought you were just going to the ladies' room.* She was nearly fluent in ASL since she'd taken lessons right along with Sara after meningitis had destroyed Sara's hearing at the age of six.

Sara circled her heart, the sign for *sorry.*

Keesha nodded at Geneva Johnson who was now ushering two men into the room. One was the smaller man Sara had seen huddled against the Sphinx minutes before.

Sphinx Man, as she thought of him, registered shock, then something she might call anxious dismay as he glanced across the room and recognized her. He turned away as Geneva Johnson spoke to him.

Keesha signed with her hands tight against her ribs, as if someone in the group might be capable of visually eavesdropping. *We get to see the collection.*

Sara's eyebrows stayed high. Keesha wasn't speaking or even mouthing the words. *Secret?* Sara asked.

Wait and see, Keesha signed.

Chapter 3

Neither of them had to wait long. Sara had to stand on tiptoes to see over the heads of the women in front of her, but as she got a clear look at Mrs. Johnson's mouth she was able to read most of her speech.

"As a thank you for your generous support and all the work you've done to organize this fabulous event, the museum and the representatives of the Eldridge Collection would like to give you a preview." She gestured over Sara's head, but Sara didn't turn around. Unlike the rest of the group, Sara remained facing forward to decipher the last of Geneva Johnson's announcement.

"The gentleman in the back of the room is Sean Riley. He's here with the collection. His partner Matthew Allen is waiting for you. If you'll follow our security coordinator, David Caldwell, you're in for a treat."

As Mrs. Johnson finished talking, Sara finally turned. It was no surprise that David Caldwell, the security coordinator, was the tall balding man with the photo ID card she'd seen upstairs. Sean Riley — she'd ask Keesha later if she'd understood the name correctly — was Sphinx Man. Caldwell left and in a moment Mrs. Johnson motioned for everyone to follow Sean Riley from the room.

Name again, Sara signed to Keesha as the men left.

"Riley and Caldwell," Keesha repeated after finger spelling all three names for her. She faced Sara so her lips could be read easily. "Mrs. Johnson just said that Caldwell will take us upstairs, too, so we can all see where the party will be set up."

Hard as she tried, Sara couldn't keep her cheeks from burning. The dreaded flush crept up from her collar. Keesha read it immediately and smiled. *Relax. She said this time the alarm system is off.*

Sara waited as Sean Riley lead them through a door marked SECURITY. She signed to Keesha. *C-A-L-D-W-E-L-L was already up there. They both were. He must have turned off the alarm while they were there, then turned it back on again when they left. Never saw me.*

It's over. Forget it, Keesha replied with a diplomatic smile.

Sara passed David Caldwell as she entered the room. After a glare that would have melted the banister cat, he turned to Riley. The room was unremarkable. There was an empty conference table in the middle and in plain view near the ceiling, lights blinked on small security cameras. Each was positioned at a different angle.

Keesha nudged Sara and pointed at them. "After what just happened, do you think we're being watched by somebody in another room?"

"The answer to that is yes," Caldwell said.

The startled volunteers looked around in confusion as he nodded at Sara and Keesha. "The girls were wondering about security. In this room, you're all on camera. Mr. El-

dridge's representatives need to be assured
that the facilities are secure."

Sara scanned the room, half expecting another drama. Instead Caldwell nodded to
Matthew Allen and Sean Riley. They lifted a
box between them from the floor to the table.
It was shaped like a small footlocker and reminded her of camp and school and the end-
less packing and unpacking she'd done over
the past ten years.

Unlike her plain, utilitarian footlockers
that had HOWELL stenciled on each side, this
was covered in smooth leather. She craned
her neck and made out the RCE monogram
embossed on the front. Brass tacks, hinges,
and corner plates gleamed. Sean Riley
opened the small locks with three sets of
keys. With all the ceremony of a royal unveil-
ing, he and Matthew Allen lifted the lid
slowly as if they knew everyone in the room
would gasp.

The first level was a padded velvet and
satin tray.

The tray was partitioned into velvet sec-
tions. There were scarab bracelets to the left,
three in single strands of different colors,

each linked with gold chain. Riley unwound a belt and held it up. Gold coins dangled from the links, each one more spectacular than the first. There were necklaces and earrings, even miniature lanterns, pottery lamps, and vases.

The room dissolved in confusion. No one attempted to touch anything, but every mouth moved, eyebrows arched, shoulders hunched as the volunteers edged each other for a closer look.

Sara turned, feeling that she was being watched. David Caldwell was standing against the door. Their eyes locked in a brief glance she couldn't decipher. His brows knit in a small gesture most would have missed. Then he gazed over her head.

Sara strained to read Sean Riley's lips. He was shaking his head. "Believe it or not, what you see here isn't the exhibit. Those trunks are still packed and locked in the museum vault. What you see here are professional reproductions, commissioned by Mr. Eldridge for his personal use. Women like yourself borrow them on occasion. Schools use them for educational programs. Some have been

used on Broadway and in Hollywood pro-
ductions that demand authenticity. Mr. Eldridge has even been known to give a few
away." Riley replaced the tray. "He has gen-
erously donated these for use during your
fund-raiser Saturday night. We've given
Geneva some small vases and lamps for use
in the centerpieces on the tables."

Sara's brown eyes widened as the room
burst into applause. No wonder Caldwell and
Sphinx Man had been giving her searching
looks. She'd already been up in restricted ter-
ritory. They probably thought she was some
reckless teenager bent on sneaking around
priceless artifacts that they were responsible
for guarding. She concentrated guiltily on
what Sean Riley was saying.

"And each of you is invited to wear replicas of what will be on display during the exhibit."

Chapter 4

"It's a necklace made from Greek coins. Each coin has a different likeness. Between about every fourth coin there's an ivory figure, all the way around my neck. The design is raised — three-dimensional — even to the clasp in the back. I'll wear my hair up so all those high-paying guests can see all of it."

Sara was in her living room trying not to rush in her excitement to describe what she'd been allowed to pick out to wear. She needed practice speaking and Steve needed practice with ASL so she was using both. She laughed at the concentration on her brother's face as he tried to catch it all.

Bret Sanderson laughed, too. Sara had

been dating the Penham School basketball player all fall. He was hearing but he had deaf parents and was fluent in ASL. Attending different schools kept them apart during the day and so far, at least, it was true that absence made the heart grow fonder.

Like Steve, Bret worried about the danger she often got herself into, trying to do police work, like Steve.

She conveniently omitted any mention of setting off alarms, or angry looks from concerned security guards as she tapped the hollow of her throat. *"A cameo sits right in the front with battling warriors on either side."* Sara dropped her hands. "Trojans on the left, I think, and the Greeks on the right. Maybe the other way around. I was so excited I wasn't paying attention. They said the Prince of Molvaria had it copied as a wedding present for his bride in 1740." *Understand?* she added again in ASL.

"I got most of it." *What about Keesha?* Steve signed *K, FRIEND,* the name sign for their neighbor.

"All Egyptian." *She gets to wear a neck piece of beads and gold that makes her look like* — Sara paused unable to sign Hatshep-sut or Cleopatra.

"Cleopatra or somebody," Steve finished for her.

"Right."

Sara and Bret were finishing a pizza before an early movie. It was their last date before Bret left with his family for vacation over the long New Year's holiday at Spruce Ridge, a resort in the mountains, two hours north of Radley.

Sara leaned back in the couch. "I wish you could be at the fund-raiser Saturday night."

"I'd be the only one there under fifty. I wish you could be skiing with me."

Steve grinned. *"She will be."*

Say again, Sara signed, sure she'd misun-derstood. Steve waved his hands around, stood up and pretended to ski.

Sara's heart jumped and she tapped her chest.

"Yes, you. Lieutenant Marino's on a case and can't take her vacation until the end of next week. I offered to sublet the condo-minium she's paid for. We'll drive up Sunday and stay through New Year's."

"Great!" Sara was still grinning in surprise.

Steve worked, worked and worked and worked. When he wasn't at his desk at the Fourth Precinct station, he was out on undercover assignments. He had the scars to prove it.

"We need the break," he was saying. "Since Dad died we haven't done much of anything but try to adjust, get on with our lives, bury ourselves in work for me, school for you. I don't even know how we survived Christmas."

Sara knew. She glanced at the corner of the living room where the Christmas tree had been. They'd had both sets of grandparents come for three days of bittersweet celebration. They'd all agreed they'd needed each other's support, but she was glad the holiday was over. The rest of school vacation had been spent with Bret and Keesha and calls on her telecommunication machine to the deaf friends she'd left behind at Edgewood. What little free time Steve had was spent with Marisa Douglas, the administrative nurse he'd met in the emergency room of the East End General Hospital.

Except for Keesha and Bret, who was leaving in the morning, Sara's friends were away and until today's snowfall, the weather had consisted mostly of frozen rain.

"New Year's Eve is Tuesday night. If Marisa can get away, she'll join us," Steve was saying.

"New Year's." Bret shook his head. *"I had no idea you might be up there. I invited Damon Miner this morning."*

Steve ran his thumb against his cheek, the sign for girl. "We have room for a friend." He signed *K, FRIEND, K, CAMERA, L, RED*, the name signs for Keesha Fletcher and Kim Roth and Liz Martinson, Sara's closest friends.

"No Kim. No Liz. They're gone with family for the whole vacation." She and Bret grinned at each other, however, as they drew the same conclusion. Keesha would be perfect. She skied; she knew Damon from the Penham basketball games, and she liked him.

They were interrupted by Tuck, Sara's

hearing-ear golden retriever who stretched, sniffed the pizza box, and trotted into the foyer.

Steve glanced at his watch. "Tuck needs to go out. Can you two walk him before your movie? I'm due to pick up Marisa in fifteen minutes."

Rain, snow . . . "Always an excuse."

He signed *M, HOSPITAL,* the name sign they'd given Marisa Douglas when she'd started dating Steve. "She's only got an hour dinner break."

Sara offered him the last slice of pizza. "Hospital food, tonight?"

He shook his head. "We're going to run over to the Side Door Cafe. I'll be at work when you get home." He patted Bret's shoulder. "See you Sunday. I'll challenge you to a run down Jackknife."

Bret laughed. "It's a deal."

By the time Sara, Bret, and Tuck reached the apartment lobby a thin blanket of snow lay over the shrubbery. Out on the street a sanding truck lumbered past. John O'Connor, the Thurston Court doorman, was in the visitors' parking area shoveling the walk that led to the entrance. It was well below freezing and the powdery flakes blew and drifted in and out of the streetlights. It made the night magical.

Sara grinned up at Bret and pulled on her gloves and knit cap, while he zipped up his parka. Tuck pulled at his leash, anxious to chase flakes. They started off in the direction of the block of shops that made up the closest commercial area. As they walked along, a familiar face caught her eye. A man was crossing the street. For a minute she couldn't place him, then it came to her. It was David Caldwell, the head of security for the Eldridge fund-raiser. As Bret turned to see what she was staring at so intently, Sara caught Caldwell's eye. He gave her the same intense look he'd given her at the museum. Something about it made her uneasy.

Chapter 5

Caldwell gave her a final searching glance, then turned to a parked Jeep as the headlight blinked and the interior light came on. She watched him get into the snowy vehicle. The light snapped off and a shot of exhaust told her the engine had started. He disappeared down the dark residential street.

Bret was looking at her as intently as Caldwell had. *Did you know that guy?*

Sara stood up and smiled sheepishly. *He's in charge of security for this show. I didn't tell you . . . I went into the gallery where the exhibit's going to be. I wasn't supposed to be up there. I set off the alarm. He and a guy from the collection were in there, too. Making plans, I guess. They must have turned the alarm back on when they left. I feel crummy about it because he looks at me like I'm a troublemaker.*

You could be. I'm sure he's got enough to worry about without thinking you're sneaking around.

I wasn't sneaking!

Bret shook his head impatiently. *Why aren't I surprised?*

Wait a minute!

Sara brushed snowflakes off his hair. *I can't help it if I'm curious.*

Just don't let it get you into trouble.

When have I ever been in trouble?

Bret threw up his hands and kissed her deeply.

At the final rehearsal before the party, once again they were ushered into the security room with the women who were running the gala. The monogrammed leather box sat on the table. A straight-faced guard stood in the corner, the only indication that security might be needed. As usual, the jewelry was handled by Sean Riley and Matthew Allen.

Matt Allen gave the women the earrings,

necklaces, or choker imitations of the priceless gems that would be on display.

After the women were settled, Sean
handed Mrs. Johnson a beaded neck piece.
She draped it around Keesha, then asked for
the Greek necklace for Sara. When the clasp
was fastened, she handed both girls a stack of
the brochures they were to hand out.

Sara paused as Mrs. Johnson knit her
brows. She motioned for Keesha and Sara to
go back to the jewelry box. "Everyone will
be looking at your hands as you give out the
brochures. Let's add some bracelets."

Riley handed Keesha three bands of
scarabs joined by gold links. For Sara they
decided on a snake design. The serpent
wound around nearly three inches of her arm.

Sara rotated her arm so the bracelet glim-
mered in the ceiling light. "Spectacular," she
said.

She touched the necklace self-consciously
as they walked along the now-familiar route
to the back staircase. She and Keesha were
the last ones on the stairs and Sara paused at
the top just long enough to show Keesha the
cat.

"Why do Egyptian artifacts always look like they're staring into the unknown?" Keesha pointed to the eyes. "This guy sees everything."

Sees all, knows all, Sara signed as she glanced around. Despite the activity, a chill was present. In the space of twenty-four hours the room had been transformed. Round tables, each with white linen cloths and eight gilt chairs, filled the perimeter. A long serving table stood against the Gothic church edifice. Keesha touched her shoulder and translated as Sara strained to read Mrs. Johnson's lips. She was turning and gesturing as she spoke, which made it all the more difficult.

She says the exhibit display cases are up. The Eldridge Collection will be laid out tomorrow morning. The party begins at six P.M. and she wants us here by five o'clock. We're to come through the employees' entrance at the back of the building.

As Keesha finished, Mrs. Johnson walked across the foyer. Even half ready, the Hall of Architecture had an air of excitement and anticipation that made Sara's skin tingle. She rotated her wrists and looked at the bracelets, suddenly aware that at least one of the uniformed security guards was watching her.

She wants us at our stations, Keesha was saying.

Keesha crossed over to the Egyptian Room and looked up warily at the Sphinxes looming on either side of the entrance. Sara smiled. Yesterday, up here alone, the hall had been eerie, but now, finally, she was caught up in the enthusiasm and expectation of the volunteers.

She read R.C. Eldridge's name in the speech of two women and guessed by their gestures that they were speculating on what he might look like or what they wanted to ask him about his collection the following evening when he'd be the guest of honor.

She stood next to the column at the arched entrance to the Greek Room and looked in at the display cases that had been moved out to the middle. The empty shelves were lighted. Sean Riley and a bearded man were busy studying the angles, tilting their heads, nodding and pointing. Sara stepped from around the column as they moved further down the room with their backs to her.

Watching them made her wonder how many plainclothes security agents would be on duty during the party. Private security detail was a job Steve had taken for extra money during his first days on the force. She could just imagine her brother blending in with the Radley elite tomorrow night.

Chapter 6

Mrs. Johnson broke Sara's reverie. "Once people arrive and start to mingle," she said when Keesha and Sara were back together, "you both may move around, too. If you stand next to your displays, I'm sure patrons will be interested in comparing your jewelry copies to the real thing." She tapped Sara's bracelet as Sara nodded that she'd understood.

Mrs. Johnson pointed to the far end of the Egyptian Room where the reproduction of a tomb entrance was flanked by a sarcophagus. "Keesha, your neck piece is very similar to the one on the mummy coffin back in the tomb. You might want to stand back there for a time."

Keesha gave her a weak nod.

When Geneva Johnson dismissed the group, Sara and Keesha led the way back down the stairs. Even as Sara crossed the room she could feel the steady gaze of a guard on her.

"It's like having your own private bodyguard," Keesha said as they reached the corridor.

"I wish I knew what he was thinking. It's as if Caldwell told each of them not to trust me. Is he afraid I'm going to run out the door with this necklace? He's been staring so much it feels creepy and secure at the same time."

"It's not you. There was a robbery of one of the pieces of the Eldridge Collection when it was in Detroit a few years ago. They're all nervous, probably. I wish the exhibit had been set up. I'm dying to see the real stuff." Keesha put her arm out and they both looked at the bracelets. "I had no idea they would be this heavy."

Sara pulled the necklace away from her neck. "Imagine how the real stuff feels."

When the guard passed them and went into the security room, Keesha signed her reply. *If we get these eagle eyes staring at us for wearing glass copies, imagine how tight the security will be tomorrow night when all of the collection is laid out in the cases.*

The temperature in Radley hovered at the freezing mark which kept the fallen snow fluffy and dry. It gave the city a magical quality. Another dusting had begun by the time Keesha drove Sara back to Thurston Court Friday night.

They left her car in the basement parking garage of their house and rode the elevator together to their seventh-floor apartments. As they walked down the hall, Keesha pulled her hand from her chest to her stomach: *Hungry? Starving.*

How about the Side Door Cafe? I'll drive, as soon as I get into some jeans.

Sara held up ten fingers and agreed. It wasn't so much hunger as the empty apartment that got her to agree. Steve was at the police station and wouldn't be home till after midnight. Tuck wasn't much good. Bret was already at Spruce Ridge. She could always count on Keesha to keep her company.

She changed quickly into a turtleneck sweater and faded jeans and hiking boots. Before she crossed the hall to the Fletchers', she went into the den. The light on the phone answering machine was steady. No messages for Steve.

She glanced out the window. Romantic, Sara thought as she looked down at the snow, except that Bret was one hundred and fifty miles north. As if her thought had triggered her telecommunications machine, the TTY light began to blink, indicating that she had a phone call. She answered and watched the display board anxiously.

It's Bret. I'm calling because I found out that there's a New Year's Eve party at the lodge. It's kind of dressy. Bring something to wear.

Okay, she typed back. **I'll scrounge around for something.** Sara added that she missed him.

I miss you, too. See you Sunday. Don't let Steve get involved in any police work that'll make you guys late.

No way. He needs the break, Sara typed and smiled. It was amazing how much

effect a quick long distance call had on lone-
liness.

Twenty minutes later she and Keesha had
managed to find an empty booth at the Side
Door, a feat that was nearly impossible when
Radley University was in session and college
students kept the cafe busy until closing time.
As they walked from the car, Sara had explained Bret's phone call and the New Year's
Eve invitation. As they ordered lasagna they
discussed what clothes to take.

While she waited for her order to arrive,
Keesha talked about what she planned to
wear on New Year's Eve. Suddenly she
stopped and looked beyond Sara.

Sara turned in her seat. She had to crane
her neck to see over the back of her booth.
Her heart thumped unexpectedly. David
Caldwell was working his way between the
tables. He reached them as Keesha shrugged
her shoulders at Sara.

"Hello." He smiled pleasantly and, without
asking, sat down next to Keesha. "I was just
finishing up as you two arrived. Excited
about tomorrow night?"

Sara nodded.

"Yes," Keesha added. "It should be a lot of fun. A lot of work for you, I guess."

Caldwell's expression stayed mild, but his eyes were dark and serious. They were accentuated by thick eyebrows in contrast to his balding scalp. It was the first time Sara had been this close to him and she was surprised by the intensity of his gaze.

He looked across the booth at Sara. "We've been busy all week, as you can imagine. Tomorrow morning the final setup goes into place."

Sara glanced at Keesha. Were they meant to make small talk about the exhibit? Despite her expertise, it was difficult to interpret his expression. She waited as he drummed his fingers on the table.

"Sara. It is Sara Howell, isn't it?"

She nodded, grateful she could read his lips.

"I know Geneva explained the importance of security for tomorrow night. Mr. Eldridge has been very precise in what he wants us to do. He's had trouble in the past. And at the Radley museum, we're just not used to dealing with special events of this magnitude. In fact, I worried that this party might put the exhibit at risk." He paused and stared over her head, still drumming his fingers. "Your exploring in the Hall of Architecture after closing hours was a case in point."

Sara opened her mouth to answer him, but he continued.

"Of course you shouldn't have been snooping around. No one was authorized to be up there. I certainly had no idea and I don't want you to misunderstand what you might have overheard while you were in the gallery. My conversations are strictly confidential, especially with Mr. Riley who represents R.C. Eldridge. We have a major patron to consider." He finally began to play with the edges of a napkin. A vein pounded in his temple.

Chapter 7

"I didn't hear anything."

Caldwell frowned at her muffled voice. His eyes widened.

Surely he knew. Anger rose in her. "Mr. Caldwell, I'm deaf." *I'm deaf.* She tapped her ear for good measure.

"What do you mean, deaf? What are you talking about?" His hands were still.

"Deaf. I read speech, but I couldn't see your lips in the gallery. I didn't hear anything." She tapped her ear again. "Your security plans are safe." She didn't take her eyes off him.

"Deaf!" his thick brows nearly melded into one wide line. Color crept up from his collar. "They said you set off the alarm, but nobody said anything about . . . Why didn't someone tell me! No one said anything." He finally leaned back. "You haven't discussed anything with that boyfriend of yours — or you?" he finished as he turned to Keesha.

Keesha said tersely, "We've only talked about what we're supposed to wear and what time to arrive tomorrow night. That's it, Mr. Caldwell."

Sara expected him to relax. He did manage a forced smile. "Deaf. Well then, I guess we're all set. . . . Sorry. This whole thing has me on edge. . . . Responsibility. This was just one of the loose ends. Enjoy your party tomorrow night." He stood up abruptly, nodded to both of them, then worked his way back through the tables to the door.

As the waitress arrived with their orders, Sara tried to calm down.

"What was that all about? He knew about Bret?" Keesha asked when they were alone.

Sara's eyes were dark with annoyance. "He's been following me! I saw him when Bret and I walked Tuck. What did he think I'd do, tell 'my boyfriend' the security plans for the party so Bret could kidnap Eldridge? I didn't sneak into the hall, either, I just walked up the staircase. He and Riley were standing next to the Sphinx." She pulled her forked index and middle finger from her eyes: *See.* "I guess I really shook him up." *Surprise. My fault. Okay! So I shouldn't have been up there. But he doesn't need to get so upset about it.*

"Do you think the museum's had threats about the exhibit?"

"Who knows? Maybe Eldridge is pressuring him to be extra careful because of the robbery in Detroit." Lost in thought, Sara ate a bite of lasagna. When she'd swallowed, she looked across her plate to Keesha. "Keesha, it wasn't just luck that he ran into us."

Keesha frowned and signed: *Say again.*

No coincidence. "First I see him on the street when I walk Tuck with Bret. Now here. He's been waiting for the right time to find out what I know."

What you know?

About his security plans or something. Sara shrugged her shoulders. "Who knows? You saw him. He's a nervous wreck. I guess the last thing he needed was me setting off alarms."

* * *

Saturday's precipitation turned from snow to drizzle as the temperature climbed into the thirties. Salt and sand trucks were out on the main roads to fight the ice, but the sun broke through by noon. To kill her nervous anticipation about the evening, Sara grabbed Tuck and took him for a walk to the Fourth Precinct police station, on the chance that Steve might be there. There was no reason to think that David Caldwell was still following her, but she looked over her shoulder all the way.

Steve was in the community room with Lieutenant Rosemary Marino, which gave Sara a chance to thank her for the surprise trip to Spruce Ridge. Both officers were dressed in worn jeans and dark, nondescript shirts.

"Undercover?" Sara asked when she finished talking about skiing. Steve nodded and Sara knew better than to ask for details. "Will you be home tonight?"

"I get off at four. Marisa might come by on her way to the hospital. She wants to see your dress."

"I wish she could see the jewelry I wear with it."

Chapter 8

The gala was a huge success. R.C. Eldridge was as tall and distinguished as Sara imagined — and never alone. Someone was always at his shoulder, shaking his hand . . . while David Caldwell hovered at a discreet distance as if determined to thwart a kidnapping attempt. Perhaps it wasn't the exhibit that had Caldwell tense, it was Eldridge. At ten P.M., after he'd made a speech and posed for photographers, the ranks closed in. Caldwell escorted the millionaire out to the waiting limousine.

Eldridge's departure was Sara and Keesha's cue that they could leave, as well. After a final look around, Matt Allen lead the two of them downstairs to the security room. As

Sara reluctantly undid the clasp of her necklace, Matt stopped her.

He smiled. "I have a surprise for you. You may keep your jewelry as a goodwill gesture."

Sara raised her wrist and tapped the bracelet, sure she'd misunderstood.

Matt nodded. "You two did all the work. We'd like you to keep the necklaces and bracelets as mementos."

Keep them? Sara signed rapidly to Keesha.

She nodded. "How do we thank Mr. Eldridge?"

"Leave that to me. I'll give him your thanks when we get back to Miami." He glanced at his watch. "I have my orders to stay upstairs with the exhibit. Enjoy your jewelry." He handed them flannel bags stamped with the Eldridge monogram.

Snowflakes danced in the security lights as they crossed the well lighted lot for the Fletchers' car that Keesha had driven.

I can't believe we can keep these. Perfect for New Year's Eve. Sara threw her arms around herself to warm up.

Lucky, Keesha signed as they reached her car. *If I wore mine I'd look like C-L-E-O at a ski lodge.*

Bring them anyway. I'm dying to show Bret.

As Keesha drove them out of the parking lot, the back wheels spun on an icy patch. She let up on the accelerator and eased the car forward.

"I hope it's not like this all the way home," Sara said as she watched the snow fly in their headlights.

Keesha nodded, but as she turned the wheel, Sara grabbed her arm. Straight ahead, caught in the beam of the headlight, was a dark bundle dusted with the fresh snowfall. Sara's heart jumped. Someone was slumped between the building and the parked cars.

Keesha jammed on the brakes sending both of them against their seat belts as the car fishtailed precariously close to a parked sedan.

"It's a person! Keesha, someone's been lying out here in the snow."

Chapter 9

Sara tried to run as she left the car, but she skidded on the ice and forced herself to slow down. She reached the body with Keesha on her heels. It was a man. He lay on his side, one arm flung out as if he'd tried to catch or balance himself. A pool of blood fanned out under him. He was covered with a thin layer of snow.

Keesha had her hand over her mouth, but managed to bend down. "I'm sure there's ice here, too, under this snow." *Ice. I'll bet he fell and cracked his head.* She pointed to the marks in the snow. Sara knelt down for a closer look. She put her hand to her face and gasped.

Recognize him?

She nodded slowly. *It's the guard from the first night, the one I surprised on the stairs.* She brushed away the snow and pressed her fingers to his neck as she prayed for a pulse. His unseeing stare and blue-tinged lips told her she wouldn't find one. *He's been dead for a while,* she finally signed as she pulled her hand away.

Slipped on the ice?

Sara was about to agree when she saw blood on the retaining wall. As she stood up for a closer look, she found a deep dent in a car beside her. She fought nausea as she nudged Keesha. Together they looked up at the roof of the museum.

He fell? From all the way up there? "We need to go for help," Keesha said. "I guess there's no point in one of us staying here."

Sara nodded slowly and turned back to the entrance. She stopped. "We can't go back to the party, it'll ruin everything." She looked around for anyone who might have seen or heard something. There was no one. The closest person was the parking attendant at the main lot. She pointed, already fighting tears. *He's close. We can get help from there and it won't wreck the party.*

Keesha signed back, *Somebody's dead and we don't want to ruin a party.*

Keesha's mother gave Sara a final hug as she and her daughter left the Howells' kitchen for their own apartment across the hall. It was nearly midnight, but Marisa Douglas offered Sara another cup of tea. Sara, thankful that Marisa had had time to stop by, took it with shaking hands and a lump still in her throat.

"What was the guard doing on the roof?" she asked for the hundredth time. "Why would they post somebody up there on such an icy night?"

"I'm sure they had their reasons," Marisa replied. She looked at the costume jewelry laid out on the table. Marisa held the necklace out in front of her. "Letting you keep these was really generous. It's so awful that the night ended on such a tragic note."

Steve hung up the phone from the call he'd placed to the police station. "You're sure you're all right?" he said to Sara. *Okay?*

Sara nodded even though tears brimmed over her lashes. "Ever since the rehearsals I've just had a creepy feeling. Uneasy. David Caldwell must be a wreck over this. It was probably his idea to station a guard on the roof in case some helicopter swooped down to kidnap Eldridge." She tried to laugh at her attempted humor, but couldn't.

Steve frowned and Sara haltingly explained Caldwell's visit to their table at the Side Door Cafe. "He was in charge of security for the night. He was trying to make everything perfect. Now this."

"The accident doesn't really have anything to do with the exhibit," Marisa offered.

Steve agreed. "At the station they said no one knows why the guard was stationed outside except that the Eldridge limousine had just left. They figured he was just checking the parking area."

"From the roof?" Sara jabbed her index finger into the air to make sure Marisa and her brother understood. "Won't this mean they'll do an autopsy, maybe an inquest?"

They all exchanged glances. Steve put his arm on Sara's shoulder. "Much as you'd like to be, you're not a cop, at least not yet. Leave this mess to the department."

"Even you think it's a mess." *You think so, too.*

"No, I didn't mean that. Right now it looks like an accident. Don't let it ruin the night for you. The party was a big success . . . and we're going on vacation. I want to get out of here tomorrow, relax and enjoy ourselves. No schoolwork for you to think about —"

"Just a dead security guard."

Steve circled his heart. "I'm as sorry as you, but it was an accident." He smiled sympathetically. "Put on that jewelry, then you can be the Greek goddess of curiosity."

Curious? Sara signed.

Marisa laughed. "Curious."

Sara lifted the necklace and let the coins dangle. "All I want is to get into my bed and dream about the ski slopes. By the way, Mrs. Johnson said the museum is predicting record crowds tomorrow when the exhibit opens to the public."

Steve yawned. "We'll drive past on our way to the interstate. See what we're missing."

"Like more dead bodies in the parking lot?" Sara added.

Not funny, Sara.

Not funny at all, she signed with a shiver.

The following morning Sara read the *Radley Gazette* while Steve took Tuck for his walk. The death of the guard, Thomas Maloney, was covered in a small column on the front page. The article was concise and referred to the death of the Radley Museum security guard as an accident, pending the results of an autopsy. It stated that he was a retired Richmond police officer who had moved to the area to be near his grown son and daughter-in-law. Sara sighed, as depressed over the fact that he was leaving family behind as she would have been if he'd been alone.

The headline article: RADLEY MUSEUM SALUTES ELDRIDGE COLLECTION took half the page. There were shots of the exhibit, Geneva Johnson, and the volunteers who had pulled the function together. In every shot of the renowned R.C. Eldridge, Sara was able to catch a glimpse of David Caldwell. *Never lets him out of his sight,* she signed to herself.

At the bottom of the page was a shot of Keesha and one of her. They were smiling with the brochures in their hands. Not a care in the world, she thought, while Thomas Maloney was lying dead in the parking lot. The caption mentioned them by name and the fact that they had been art students at the museum. She scanned the copy for mention of the death of the guard in the main article but there wasn't any. Mustn't ruin anyone's perception of the party. She closed the paper.

By noon Sara and Keesha had helped Steve pack his Jeep with their suitcases and groceries. Their skis were on the roof rack. Keesha's brother Marcus had agreed to take care of Tuck and Sara gave her dog a final furry hug before she climbed into the backseat with Keesha. Marisa was waiting at her apartment. When they'd added her skis and luggage, they left Radley by way of the museum, as Steve had promised.

As they reached the museum complex, Sara gasped at the crowd that formed a single line down the steps of the entrance and onto the sidewalk. The sun was out but the December wind was raw.

"Will you look at the crowd, even in the cold! What a moneymaker for the museum," Keesha said and signed as she tapped Sara's shoulder to get her attention.

ELDRIDGE COLLECTION had been lettered onto a banner draped over the entrance to the Hall of Architecture. It snapped and fluttered as the wind worked up under it.

Sara pointed. *"Look at the banner. It's attached up at the roof line. Maybe the guard was up there checking on the fastenings or something."*

Marisa looked at Steve then around to Sara. "Steve says since we're here, he wants you to show him where you found the body. Always the cop," she added with a wink.

Sara pointed and Keesha directed Steve around to the back of the building. The back lot was nearly full. Keesha pointed to the granite retaining wall, half expecting to find yellow crime scene tape blocking off the area.

Steve drove the car slowly through the lot,

then turned back toward the exit. Sara sat up and put her hand on his shoulder. "Stop here. I want to show you the spot."

"I'm off duty. This is close enough for me."

Come on. We're already here. She didn't wait to see if her brother had understood her. She already had one foot on the pavement.

The four of them hunkered against the wind and crossed to the wall.

"Here." Sara pointed, then shaded her eyes and scanned the roof line. "Maybe he had to fix the banner. I never thought of that."

"It's as good an explanation as you're likely to get," her brother replied. He hooked his arms through the elbows of both girls. "Help me get them back, Marisa, or we'll never ski."

Marisa laughed but as they all turned back to the car, Sara looked over her shoulder.

The retaining wall was chest-high, built up against a grassy slope that rimmed the edge of the building. Snow covered the lawn and most of the wall. Sara worked her arm free from Steve and went back to where she'd knelt the night before. Something . . . something . . .

She was as cold as the other three, but she pretended not to understand that they were calling her to hurry. Deafness had its advantages. She turned so she couldn't read their lips.

The space where the dented car had been was vacant. A gust caught the snow on the hill and blew it over the crimson stain on the wall. Maloney's blood had stained the cement. Enough. She shuddered, ready to join the others. This time as she turned to them, the toe of her boot hit something in the snow. A handgun skittered over the pavement.

Chapter 10

Nausea knotted her stomach. The gun was barely visible now and would have been hidden the night before by the bumper of the car that had broken Thomas Maloney's fall from the roof.

"Steve!" She had no idea whether she had screamed or whether it was her expression that brought him running. Marisa reached her before she could kneel. She knew better than to touch the gun.

Forty-five minutes later, the four of them were still sitting in the main security office of the museum. A bank of closed-circuit televisions monitored the collections under the watchful eyes of a set of guards. Sara barely noticed them. She was lip-reading the police sergeant who had taken a statement from Steve.

"Wouldn't someone have noticed last night if Maloney's gun were missing from his holster?" Steve asked.

"You'd think so," the sergeant replied. "We've got a call into the guy in charge last night. Day off, poor sucker."

"I know how he feels," Steve replied.

Sara explained again about the location and the parked cars that had been nosed up against the wall during the party. Steve frowned and muttered something to the officer about playing detective and vacation. "I don't want to get involved with this, but I guess we'd better give you our phone number."

Steve's sour expression told Sara he hated giving the police the number in Spruce Ridge, but it was Keesha and Sara who had to be reachable if there were any more questions.

This is definitely not what I had in mind for the first hours of vacation, he signed as he got back into the Jeep.

* * *

It was nearly three o'clock by the time they crossed the Buckeye River and left Radley. They headed north on the interstate.

It was still sunny, but the wind blew snow squalls down from the mountainous terrain as they drove further north toward the peaks. Sara looked out the window and tried to concentrate on the days ahead, the beauty of the foothills . . . anything that would take her mind off the picture of Thomas Maloney lying dead in the snow.

He must have drawn his gun first.

Maybe he had been using the butt end to hammer in the banner fastenings. Maybe the gun was unrelated. Even Steve would agree that a tossed weapon could have come from anywhere — or nearly anybody.

At five o'clock Steve took the exit that brought them over the crest of the hill that opened onto the Spruce Ridge vista. In the dark gray winter light, designated ski trails for night skiing were already bright under floodlights fastened to the lift line poles.

As they drove through the ski town of Colby, and further into the mountains, dry crystalline flakes danced in the headlights of the Jeep. The kind that had swirled and danced and finally drifted over Thomas Maloney as he lay undiscovered in the museum parking lot, Sara thought. She gritted her teeth and stared through the windshield, willing herself to focus on what lay ahead, not what they'd left behind.

Alpine Village had been cleverly designed so that a single road wound its way from the lodge and inn at the base of the mountains up to the slopeside complex. The modern units hugged the hillside in clusters like upturned shoeboxes, all angles and decks, each placed for maximum view. Steve found 407 without any trouble.

He parked the Jeep in front of the two-story unit and they hauled in their luggage. Steve claimed the bedroom and loft at the top of the stairs. Sara crossed the combined living and dining room and pulled open the draperies. Sara stared out at the silent winter scene. She watched as a few of her neighbors skied by and she tried to share Keesha's enthusiasm.

Keesha hadn't wandered where she shouldn't have, hadn't met Thomas Maloney face-to-face, hadn't fought the foreboding for two days. Nevertheless, they'd been through the worst of it together and if Keesha were bothered even a fraction as much as Sara by what had happened, she wasn't letting it show.

Cheer up, Keesha signed as if she'd read Sara's mind. *This is our big adventure. Put the rest behind you,* she added with a smile.

Sara grinned back at her, weakly. It helped.

Marisa had already begun to unpack in her bedroom, so Sara and Keesha moved their luggage into the twin-bedded room that looked out over the parking area in the front. Keesha plugged in the TTY. Steve set their skis in the rack at the front door. The minute they were organized, the four of them descended on the kitchen. Sara insisted that they eat with the draperies open.

"I feel like some skier's going to appear from the woods, clomp up to the window, and ask for a bite," Marisa said as she looked at the deck.

"At least it's somebody we know," Sara replied. She laughed and pointed at familiar figures working their way across the trail. Bret and Damon Miner stomped the final distance to the edge of the deck. Keesha opened the slider and let them in.

The blast of frigid air was followed by a bear hug as Bret swung Sara around. As he finally unzipped his parka he introduced Damon to Steve and Marisa who insisted that they join them at the table.

"Great conditions. Snowed all day yesterday. Fabulous powder. I gave up snowboarding so we could do North Face this afternoon." As Bret signed and spoke Steve got up from the table. Bret pantomimed to Sara that the phone was ringing.

Police news, she thought. More questions for Keesha and me. Gun questions. Gun answers. She looked at Bret so she could follow his skiing conversation, but she kept an occasional glance on Steve who stood at the wall phone frowning and shaking his head.

Keesha turned. "For me?" She went to the phone.

Steve signed and spoke as he returned to

the table. "It's John Fletcher." *On the phone.* "Their apartment was broken into some time late this afternoon, while we were on the road. They think whoever it was tried to get into ours, too."

Chapter 11

Sara strained to read Steve's speech as he struggled with unfamiliar ASL. Finally she waved him off and looked at Bret so he could translate every word. *"They were out,"* Bret continued as he looked at Steve. *"M-A-R-C-U-S took Tuck for a walk and bought a soda. When they got back to your floor, M-A-R-C-U-S stopped at the incinerator room to put the can in the recycling bin. M said Tuck started barking like crazy and ran down the hall to the apartments. Doors were locked to both. When M-A-R-C-U-S went into his, he discovered stuff had been moved. The VCR and stereo were on the living room floor —"* Bret glanced over at Keesha. *"Steve says*

*they're asking her what jewelry she brought
so they know if anything was actually taken."*

"Was jewelry stolen?"

Steve shook his head and continued as
Bret interpreted. *"As far as they can tell
everything is still there. Our front door
looked like it had been worked on, but not
opened. They think Tuck scared the guy. Whoever it was made the elevator or the fire stairs
and got away."*

Sara's alarm deepened as she looked at
Steve. "Do we have to go back to Radley?"

Steve shook his head. "Nothing's been
stolen. Even the Fletchers agreed there's no
point in cutting the vacation. It's short
enough as it is."

Keesha returned to the table visibly
shaken. "They went through my room, too. I
didn't bring anything with me but the silly
stuff from the museum." She shuddered.
"Thank goodness for Tuck. He saved everything." She took a swallow of soda and
looked at Sara. "Other news. David Caldwell
came by. Mom said he was worried about us
after the police told him we found the body.

He said Maloney was on the roof fixing
banner."

"What roof? What body!" Bret's facial
pression was enough to make Sara's hea
jump.

"I'll explain."

Bret looked helplessly at Steve who described what had happened. "Sara, you might
as well tell him about the gun," he threw in.
He shrugged at both boys. "There's something about my sister and trouble —"

No trouble! Sara signed.

This time Keesha quickly did the explaining, until the gun incident sounded innocu-
ous and unrelated. "Anyway," she finished,
"Caldwell wanted to make sure we were all
right and sends his sympathy. When Marcus
said we were out here he said to relax and
enjoy the skiing. He said we did a wonderf
job at the party."

Sara circled her heart. "That was nice
him. I'm sure he feels terrible about the
dent."

Bret looked grim. "Somebody died
middle of the party?"

"In the middle of the parking lot. We found him when we left," Sara added. Tears were in her eyes.

Bret arched his eyebrow as Sara hurried into the bedroom and scooped the flannel bags with the Eldridge monograms from the dresser. Since they'd met in the fall she and Bret had had more than one argument, even a breakup, over the danger she'd put herself in. She was anxious to get him off the subject.

"They let you keep this?" Damon asked.

Keesha laughed. "Pretty neat, huh? It's not priceless or anything, but it's fun and spectacular looking. We thought we'd wear these to the New Year's Eve party."

Bret picked up the serpent bracelet while Damon and Keesha examined the beaded neck piece. The boys made Keesha put it on over her sweatshirt. She stood in a model's pose. "You should have seen me in eye makeup — out to here." She arched her eyebrows and dragged her index finger from the corner of her eye to her temple. "A regular Cleopatra."

Sara put the winding snake on her arm. Her friends' gestures over the jewelry made it

easy to decipher the meaning of their conversation. She began a simple version of a snake dance while Keesha made up a rendition with Egyptian moves. The silliness raised her spirits and Sara was in the midst of twirling when she realized Marisa, then the boys, had turned their heads. Keesha stopped dancing and Sara bumped into her.

Not until she regained her balance did she realize that Steve had answered the door. He was standing in the vestibule with a guy about his own size in his late twenties. He was dressed like the rest of them in jeans and a casual sweater.

Sara's face flamed as they walked toward her.

His startled expression changed to laughter as Steve said something and led him into the kitchen. Her brother was introducing him briefly, but she couldn't read Steve's speech from her angle. Instead she shrugged and turned back to the boys.

Bret signed, *Steve said he's a neighbor looking for a can opener. He liked your dance.*

Very funny. Name?

The stranger was already headed back to the door as Bret grabbed a pen from the message pad by the phone and scribbled out CHRIS WHEELER in block letters. *He told Steve he saw us arrive so he knew there were people over here. Steve asked him to stay. Couldn't. He was in a rush — cooking dinner. Only needed the can opener.*

Just stayed long enough to see Keesha and me acting like idiots.

Bret chuckled. *Didn't bother me any.*

Sara and Keesha put their jewelry away and agreed it was time to explore Spruce Ridge. Diversion was exactly what Sara decided she needed, a chance to get caught up in the excitement of Spruce Ridge on a New Year's holiday.

Without the sun the temperature had dropped into the teens, but Bret convinced Keesha and Sara that the skiing was even better under the lights. "Besides," he added, "there's a huge fireplace in the lodge and you can warm up after every run if you feel like you can't keep up with me."

"I can keep up with you any day," she joked.

"We'll see about that."

* * *

The only problem with skiing was communication. Unless Sara took off her gloves, signing was nearly impossible and unless she stopped and looked directly at whoever was speaking, it was hard to catch the conversations in the dark. While she was here she intended to practice more lipreading.

Once everyone had dressed and put on their skis, she fell into a comfortable silence as the six of them used cross-country techniques to glide from the townhouses over the logging road and into the woods. The path was dark, but short enough so that the illuminated slopes on the other side of the pines were clearly visible. Bret bent into the hill and led the way single file along the trail. It was the perfect warmup, and a minute later they had all schussed out onto the wide, well lighted lower half of the lift line where hundreds of guests were enjoying the night skiing.

They went into the lodge and arranged for their holiday passes. The lodge was typically rustic and Sara could feel the vibrations in

her legs as skiers and snowboarders thumped
and clopped over the wooden floor in their
unlatched or unlaced ski boots.

Bret pointed to a poster advertising the
New Year's Eve party. *Next door at the inn*,
he signed. *No ski boots over there.*

Sara gestured toward the panorama outside the windows. *Will there still be night skiing?*

Damon and Keesha arrived so they
switched to speech. "There will be a big
show at midnight. The ski patrol sweeps the
slopes . . . torches, patterns with the light.
They say it's wonderful." He brushed his
closed hands into the air on either side of his
head, the sign for *wonderful.* Damon tried the
sign and Sara gave him a thumbs-up gesture.

"I think they'll keep the skating open,"
Damon added. He showed Keesha the lighted
pond that curved in front of the inn next to
two sets of paddle tennis courts. Someone
was tending a small bonfire and grill, and
there was as much activity there as on the
slopes.

"Time's wasting," Steve said as he finally
arrived with the passes. The minute Sara had

stuck hers on her zipper, she nodded toward the crowds through the window. More than anything, she wanted to throw off the gloom that had plagued her and jump feetfirst into the festival atmosphere of Spruce Ridge.

When everyone was ready, they worked their way back to the triple chairlift. Bret slung his arm around her. "Feeling okay?"

She nodded.

"Sorry about the break-in in your building," he said slowly and distinctly. "But look at it this way. You found a body. You found a gun. Your apartment was tampered with. You know that old superstition: Things happen in threes. The worst is over." He tapped his gloved hand at his temple and she nodded that she understood.

She smiled as the chairlift swung up behind them. She, Bret, and Marisa grabbed the first one with Damon, Keesha, and Steve right behind. This was no time to correct Bret by pointing out that she considered the body and the gun one event. The incident at Thurston Court had been the second. There hadn't been a third . . . yet.

Chapter 12

Sara practiced her speech. Damon had some trouble understanding her, but by the end of the second run, she was making herself understood. She had to concentrate, and concentration kept her focused.

The cold ride up the chairlift was invigorating. Snow showers blew in gusts that suddenly obliterated the stars. Just as suddenly the cloud would pass and twinkling would resume in the deep purple sky. Night skiing was confined to the broad trails under the floodlights around the lifts and the smaller trails that branched out through the woods on either side.

At the top of the triple chairlift, they had a choice of Longview and other open slopes or

Lullaby, an old logging road that ran out and back across the harder trails. It traversed the mountain close to a forty-five degree angle, making it easier and longer.

They all agreed to save the advanced trails until morning when the visibility was better and Steve, Marisa, Keesha, and Sara had had a chance to practice.

As they got off the chair, each of them had to scramble for balance in the temporary snow squall. Sara waited as Bret and Damon talked and nodded. Steve turned to Keesha and Sara. "Lullaby, this time," he said.

Cold and anxious to get her blood running, Sara bent her knees and dug in with her poles. Lullaby, marked by a green circle, the easiest of the trails, was straight ahead. She snapped her ankles together, and kept her skis parallel. The wind whipped against her cheeks until she reached the shelter of the overhanging pines. Once she was in the woods she traded the snow showers for darkness. The pines that separated her from the open slopes weren't more than twenty feet tall, she could see the fluorescent glow of the floodlights, but here, deep in the trees, she was plunged back into the shadows. She maneuvered a curve then stopped and waited for the others. No one followed.

The chill dug in. Lullaby. She was sure Steve had said it. Lullaby? Longview? She shivered. Could she have misread him? She said both out loud. There was a distinct possibility that she had. She swore silently and tapped her hand against her ski pole.

When no one appeared in the next minute, she began to shiver. It was too cold to stand and wait. The rest of the group must have skied past the trail opening and missed her as the snow flew in their faces. She was too far down the slope to hike back up, and too cold to stand in the shadows for much longer. She pulled off her gloves and swung her hands at her sides to get her circulation going, then pushed off.

No one had mentioned what to do if they got separated, but common sense told her the best place to wait would be in the bright lights of the lift line at the bottom of the mountain. With warmer hands but chilled bones, Sara picked up speed.

The trail grew from dim to dark as she

skied. There were areas where the white glow of the snow-packed path was the only way she could tell she was still on the trail. Her heart began to thump painfully. A knot formed in her stomach. She was headed away from the lift line which meant she must be going toward Alpine Village. Soon, she thought. It couldn't be much further until she'd turn that corner and the ski trail would lead her back toward civilization.

Fear began to play tricks. Besides her pounding pulse, adrenaline made her want to rush, and she tucked to increase her speed. She hadn't thought about how foolish it was to race on a dark deserted slope rimmed in pines until she caught an edge and fell. She skidded and rolled fifteen feet down the trail, kicking up snow as she finally came to rest in the powder at the edge of the trees. That's one way to get down the hill, she thought sullenly as she stood up and scooped snow out of her collar. Stupid.

She hated depending on the light at this time of night. Her deafness heightened her visual perception, but nothing helped when everything was wrapped in shadows. Maybe someone had called her as she'd set off. Maybe the chairlifts made noise in the night. Maybe if she could hear, the sounds of skiers would tell her how much further she had to ski to find Bret and Keesha.

Just perfect. Sit here in the snow and depress yourself further, she thought sarcastically. What she didn't need was more worry — or hypothermia. She dusted herself off, spit snow from her mouth and scraped it out of her hat. She leaned into the snow and reset her boot into the binding. There was a clearing less than thirty feet in front of her and from the glow, she realized she had reached the edge of the condominium complex. Relief washed through her. She could see the pattern of light. It came from the condos, glowing like welcome signs as she shook herself off. She thought briefly of skiing back home, but abandoned the idea. The rest of the group would wait — and worry.

Instead Sara positioned her poles carefully and worked herself into a standing position. Wherever you are, guys, wait for me, she ordered in the still, cold night. Wait for me. She swung her hands again and straightened up, about to push off, when motion caught her eye. Ahead of her at the hairpin turn where the trail opened to the condominiums, a figure was struggling with the depth of the snow. Skis and the packed trail had kept Sara on top, but this person was sinking to his knees with every step. He needed snowshoes.

Sara frowned. He appeared to have wandered from the condominiums into the wooded area. No skis, no poles. She watched yellow light stream along the snow beside him and realized he was swinging a flashlight. Whoever it was had a skull cap pulled low on his forehead and he hunkered against the cold in dark, nondescript clothes. With the exception of a red stripe across the shoulder area of his jacket, there was nothing unusual to identify him.

Chapter 13

Sara watched him struggle through the powder until he reached the packed trail again. She was about to hail him by skiing over, but as she positioned her poles, he beamed the flashlight ahead of himself, into the woods. She wished she had her own light. As she watched, he sank to his thighs as he plowed his way into the pines until his beam of light washed the front of what looked like a small building.

Ski patrol. Maybe the person was checking a pump house or equipment shed. He went up to the single window. The beam of light danced over the shingles and into the window. Just as suddenly the streak of light stretched out across the snow and onto tree trunks. Whoever it was had turned around.

This time Sara leaned back into the shadows and watched him trudge back through the snow, onto the packed trail, and across to the townhouses.

Sara shook out her skis and pushed off for the lodge. She squinted at the dark structure as she passed but without a flashlight, it was nearly impossible to see much of anything. If she hadn't watched the mysterious figure, she never would have known there was anything in the woods.

Enough! she told herself and continued safely along the marked trail. One more curve and the sky brightened. The spindly pines were suddenly silhouetted against the artificial glare of the floodlights and she raced down the hill.

She scanned the skiers for familiar faces and found two recognizable figures at the chairlift — Bret and Steve next to each other, throwing their arms around themselves to keep warm. Sara skidded into view and prepared for the lecture she knew would come. She wasn't disappointed.

"I thought you said Lullaby," Sara said as distinctly as possible. She tapped her ear for good measure.

Steve replied angrily with a poke of his pole at the open slope. "I said Longview. It's dark. It's late. I was ready to send out the ski patrol —"

She spread her arms. "Sorry I took the wrong trail, but they lead to the same place. Here I am. Safe. All in one piece. Nice run."

And twice as long, Bret replied with his ungloved hands. *We've been waiting and freezing. The others are inside.* He nodded toward the lodge.

She took her gloves off and held them between her teeth. *Okay. I could use some warming up, too. So, please get off my back.* She followed them into the lodge. Timing was everything where her brother and her boyfriend were concerned. This was not the time to tell either of them that she'd been alone on a dark trail within inches of someone sneaking to a deserted cabin in the woods off the old logging road.

Sara waited for tempers to cool as she went into the ski lodge with Bret and Steve on either side of her. As they pushed through the swinging doors she spotted Keesha, Damon, and Marisa at the fireplace. They were slouched on a picnic bench facing the flames with their parkas piled on the table behind them. Comfortable, Sara thought, and not at all worried about where she might have been.

"I knew you'd show up," Marisa quipped with an I-told-you-so glance at Steve. "Your brother was convinced you'd been buried in a snowdrift or dragged off to some lunatic's deserted cabin."

Sara's pulse gave an involuntary leap and when Bret suggested hot drinks, she offered to go with him to the snack bar.

"I did see somebody walking into the woods," she said when they were across the room. "Plowing through the powder with a flashlight."

"Skier off the trail?"

"No. He was walking on Logger's Run from the condominiums, then went into the woods. Odd. The snow was hip-deep. He plowed his way into the pines." Sara glanced around, blanketed suddenly with the feeling that she was being watched. The room was humming with activity. Skiers came and went around her. Faces were animated, flushed with the cold. The floor shook with the thudding of heavy boots. She had no idea what she thought she'd see. No one lounged against a table staring at her. No one lurked at the pay phone covertly cupping the mouthpiece. The Spruce Ridge base lodge looked like exactly what it was: a popular resort during a busy holiday. She scanned the room for a dark parka with a red stripe.

"What is it?" Bret asked as he followed her glance.

"A feeling, that's all."

Bret fought his annoyance. "If you have some reason to think you're in danger then we should tell Steve —"

Talk to my brother?

Yes.

Sara shook her head. She wouldn't call it danger, exactly. *I'm being silly, I guess. I just let my imagination go crazy while I was out on the trail by myself.*

Bret hugged her. "No more of that, either."

Fine with me!

"Stop worrying," he continued. "Whoever you saw had a reason for what was going on. It's none of your business. If it makes you feel better, we can take a look in the morning." Bret tapped his forehead.

She nodded that she'd understood and smiled weakly. "Okay. You're right. Things will probably make sense in the daylight."

Their orders were ready. Steve took the cups of steaming cocoa and coffee on a tray and headed back to the fireplace. A final jolt of anxiety sent fresh chills through Sara as she followed. Across the room a figure in a dark parka pushed through the doors. She put her arm out to Bret just as the figure turned. It was a tall teenager who looked about thirteen with long blond hair peeking from her ski hat. The parka had an iridescent design across the front, pink to purple.

"What?" Bret asked.

Sara managed a laugh. "Nothing."

She had cocoa loaded with marshmallows. By the time she'd finished her drink the blanket of fear had lifted. Nothing sinister was going on in Spruce Ridge. She would ruin the holiday for everybody if she kept this up. She turned to her drink and gradually fatigue replaced the anxiety.

Rather than ride the lift and ski Lullaby to Logger's Run and Alpine Village, they all agreed to take the shuttle bus that ran from the lodge to the condos. They rode back up the mountain with other vacationers, skis and poles in pockets attached to the exterior of the bus. Sara sat with Bret.

"Relax," he said when they were alone. "You've been through a scare, Sara, two scares, okay? That was back in Radley, hundreds of miles from here."

Sara nodded and looked out the window. The museum guard's funeral would take place while they were skiing. The six of them would be racing up and down the slopes of Spruce Ridge while Thomas Maloney was being buried. Maybe he'd had plans for New Year's Eve. She thought of her father's funeral, then turned back to Bret.

He smiled and signed. *This place is magical. I'm really glad you're here. It wouldn't be the same without you. That's why I don't want you to worry about what you left behind. Forget about it. It's all dead and buried.*

Chapter 14

Dead and buried. *I'll try.* She brought her thumb and fist along her cheek and out in front of her: *Tomorrow?*

Stop by for Damon and me in the morning. My parents want to say hello.

She nodded. The lifts opened at nine A.M. and she wanted to be ready. If the trail through the snow to the cabin was obvious, she'd point it out to Bret and the others. Otherwise, she agreed with Bret. She was here to party, not worry herself into a frazzle over nonexistent troubles.

The group had a flawless day of skiing on Monday, and Tuesday, New Year's Eve day, seemed full of promise. Everything that had been draped in shadows on Sunday night was gleaming under clear, hard winter skies. The sun was bright and topping the trees as everyone ate and dressed at the Howells'.

When they were ready, as agreed, Sara, Keesha, Steve, and Marisa trooped down the hill to the furthest cluster of units where Bret was staying. Both his parents were deaf and they signed to Sara and let Bret interpret their ASL for the others. The Sandersons chatted briefly about the night's celebration, then waved the group off as the six of them skied over to the waiting trails.

Unlike Sunday night the wooded trail was clear. One by one they pushed off and began the gentle descent along the old logging trail to Lullaby.

There were other skiers on the trail and Sara hoped it seemed natural for her to pause and wait. She pretended to adjust her boot as Bret signaled for the others to keep going. Once again she pulled off her gloves and shoved them in her pockets.

Since we're this close, I just want to show you what I saw the other night. Follow me. I fell over there by the tree. The person I told you about walked — no skis — through the snow from the village and came right past me with a flashlight.

Not everybody skis, Sara.

She pointed with her pole. Although Lullaby was compacted and groomed, at the place where she pointed was the unmistakable trail of disturbed snow where the figure had pushed through. The woods were thick with bare branched maples as well as the needled pines. The cabin was barely visible since snow had drifted more than halfway up the sides.

Bret grinned and pointed to the bare maple trees. *Sugar house.*

She shook her head. *No, no. He went into woods, into snow to his knees, really pushing. He left the trail. I saw the beam of his flashlight hit something. He didn't stay long. Then he went back the way he'd come.*

Bret laughed. *This is an old logging road that ran up through the mountain for timber and sugar maples.*

Say again.

S-U-G-A-R. That's a sugar house. Didn't you see shop signs when you drove through

*town? Colby's famous for its maple sugar
candy and syrup. The tourists buy tons of it.
In the spring as soon as the sap starts running they combine spring skiing with a big
sugar festival. Spruce Ridge Sugar Days. The
brochures are in the lodge. Come on, Sara,
this corner of the state makes enough to com-
pete with Vermont.*

*They don't make it in December . . . in the
dark.* She glared at his exasperated expression.

*Maybe someone was checking to make
sure the house hadn't been vandalized by
skiers. Maybe kids broke in this winter. Who
knows. It's none of your business. Don't even
think about getting yourself tangled up in another —*

She pushed his hands down. *Okay. I hope
you're right. It was just that in the dark, just
the beam of the flashlight . . .*

She laughed as he bent over and kissed her.
The last thing she wanted on this beautiful
morning with a fabulous night ahead was a
fight with Bret. No more arguments. No more
breakups. His kiss told her his mood was still
light, but the look in his eyes was serious.

Have you told Steve or Keesha?

No.

Nobody else gets to worry over your over-active imagination but me? You promised, Sara.

Okay, okay. I just wanted you to see what I saw.

I did. Now let's catch up. We'll miss the others if we don't get out of here.

Sara grabbed her gloves and pushed off. Bret had a good point. She didn't need any more excitement in her life. A dead security guard with a dropped revolver and an attempted break-in were enough for any vacation.

Unlike the day before, the slopes were crowded with the holiday skiers. Although the temperature hovered at freezing, it was far warmer under the cloudless skies and it didn't take more than two runs for Sara to realize that she'd overdressed. Her long underwear clung to her until she was miserable. When she explained that she was going back to the condo to get rid of the extra layer, they agreed to ski Longview so she could find them easily when she got back. This time she made sure she understood.

The flat trek from the edge of the logging road across the field to the condominiums made her hotter than ever. When she'd finally poled her way to the back deck, she couldn't wait to get out of the underwear that stuck to her from neck to wrists and ankles.

She unfastened her bindings, propped her skis against the deck, and walked around to the front of the condominium. The neighbor from Sunday night was going up her walk. Chris Wheeler? She tried to recall what Bret had said his name was. Once again he was in jeans and a heavy sweater, no jacket.

Sara waved her arm, hesitant as always to use her voice. He didn't see her. Trotting in ski boots felt like trying to move in cement shoes, but she finally clopped up the walk. He was already at their entrance. It was difficult to tell from the angle, but she could have sworn that he put his hand on the knob and tried to open the door, rather than ring the bell or knock.

Chapter 15

As Sara moved clumsily up behind him, he spun around. He tried to mask his surprise, but she was a master at reading expressions. His was shock, unpleasant surprise, and a good portion of anger. His already flushed complexion deepened.

"Did you hear me?" She pointed to her boots.

He forced a smile. "Never heard a thing. I was just about to return the can opener. I thought you all were out skiing. I was going to leave it in the kitchen if the door was unlocked."

Sara was tempted to ask who in their right mind would leave their condominium unlocked while they skied all day. Instead she put her hand out and waited while he pulled the can opener from his pocket.

"Thanks. Thanks a lot," he said.

"You're welcome." She put the key in the lock and turned the knob, but when he didn't leave, she stopped. Did he think she was inviting him in? She looked beyond him. "You ought to get out there. The skiing is great today."

He nodded, but he didn't look as though he'd understood. Now close up and in the daylight she took a closer look at him. His fair complexion was slightly sunburned. This close she could also see that the tanner shades in his complexion stopped along his jaw, as if he'd recently shaved off a beard.

"Are you from Radley?" she said as clearly as possible.

"Radley? No. I drove down from Milton."

"You look familiar. I thought I'd seen you around the university or something. Side Door Cafe?"

"Sorry. Somebody else."

She gave him a blank stare and weak smile, as though she hadn't understood. It was a ploy she saved for getting herself out of situations. She wasn't about to stand on her doorstep and make conversation with a guy she didn't trust in the first place. This time she added a simple good-bye, opened the door, and let herself in.

Once she was on the other side of the door, she tugged off her boots and headed for the bedroom. As she stripped off her clothes she looked out the window. She still had no idea which unit was Chris Wheeler's, but he was in the parking lot, opening the door of a sleek red sports car. It had no ski rack and certainly wasn't big enough to fit a pair inside. That wasn't all that caught her attention. He'd pulled on a jacket. It was black with a red stripe across the shoulder.

I suppose you don't want to know that the guy who borrowed our can opener is the one I saw in the woods Sunday night.

When did you see somebody in the woods?

Sara was in the triple chair with Bret and Steve. The lift had stopped and they were swaying fifty feet above Jackknife. She turned to Steve. *Sunday night when I took the wrong trail. It's a long story.*

"Short story," Bret said as he pulled off his gloves to sign as he spoke. *"She saw somebody walk with a flashlight from the condos into the woods to a sugar house."*

"And just now when I went back to change, he returned our can opener and got into a car. No ski rack. No skis. He's walking around the townhouses during the day."

Bret tapped her shoulder. *"Maybe he keeps his skis here all season and took the rack off the car. If he doesn't ski, maybe he's here to play paddle tennis like my parents, or skate or check on his maple sugar company. Did you ever think of that? Maybe he owns it."*

Sara looked at both of them. She knew what she'd promised. She really wanted to have fun like the rest of them. However, all the logic in the world didn't explain a sugar house by flashlight, and no matter how hard Chris Wheeler had tried to make it seem normal, a guy trying to get into their condo didn't feel any more logical than a security guard using the butt of his service revolver to hammer down a banner on an icy roof in the dark.

With a jolt the lift cables began to move again and they rode further up the mountain. She watched the skiers below them and then glanced from Bret to Steve. She could insist on following her intuition and work herself into an angry impasse with them, or she could ski her brains out. Sara gave up. She wasn't in danger; nobody she knew felt threatened, and she couldn't have explained if they did. Her fingers were freezing and she didn't want to spoil what so far had been a perfect day.

The day stayed perfect. Despite the crowds, the skiing was fantastic and the conditions stayed good. They tackled the moguls on Jackknife and Last Chance, outraced each other across the open slopes. At four o'clock they rode the triple chairlift together one last time. Bret and Damon were going to switch to snowboarding again. Marisa had coerced Steve into a final run, then time on the skating rink. Sara and Keesha wanted time to nap and shower before they changed for New Year's Eve.

The group separated at the top of the

mountain. Sara and Keesha skied out along Lullaby. When they reached the hairpin turn, they skied over to Logger's Run for the final stretch that led back to the condominium.

"Show me where the guy went into the woods," Keesha said as they rounded the bend and stopped.

Sara lifted her pole and pointed to the trees. "Right in there." They sidestepped in their skis to the opening between two maple trees.

Keesha leaned on her poles and squinted in the direction of the sugar house, then turned to face Sara. "I know he was out here in the dark and everything, but it doesn't seem too creepy. The guy plowed through the snow. If you were up to something illegal wouldn't you pick some place you could get to without leaving a trail even a moose could follow?"

Sara nodded and turned her skis for home. Even she was getting tired of thinking about it.

Long, hot bath, then nap, Keesha signed as Sara unzipped her parka.

Sara laughed. *For me, nap then shower.*

As Keesha disappeared into the bathroom, Sara brushed out her hair and fastened it with a barrette. Bret thought it looked glamorous piled up and the style would show off the coin necklace, which she would wear tonight.

She was tired, but it was a good tired. The exercise had made her feel alive and she had been with all the people she cared about most. She flopped down on her bed and tucked her arms under her head. The silence was comfortable. Maybe Keesha was right: a soaking bath would be better than a shower. She stared at the ceiling and drifted off.

A feeling as much as a shadow made her turn her head. Visual acuity they called it in the deaf world. Sara always thought it was more like a sixth sense. She rolled on her side and looked through the open bedroom door into the hallway. Nothing moved, but her heart hammered. Her pulse jumped. She sat up and stared.

Chapter 16

Nothing. She tiptoed across the carpeting and into the tiled hall. Nothing seemed disturbed. Beams of afternoon sun slanted through the sliders from the deck. The condo was as bright and cheerful as when they'd come in, but it didn't keep her hands from turning clammy.

Sara scanned everything until she came to the utility closet. The door was ajar. Had it been that way when they'd come in? Had she noticed as Keesha stood in front of it and pulled off her parka?

Sara took a deep breath and yanked the door open. She stared at the hot water tank and combination washer/dryer. The space between the two appliances was big enough for someone to fit into. If someone had come in . . . if someone had been caught by their early arrival, it would be a perfect place to wait for a chance to escape.

She tried to calm herself down. They'd all tease her about her imagination for this one. She opened the washing machine. Her jeans from yesterday were just where she'd thrown them, but on top was a sweater of Steve's. That was it. Steve had been in the utility closet, so it was probably Steve who'd left the door ajar. She went back to the bedroom and tried to decide whether it was worth mentioning to Keesha when she got out of the bath.

Keesha shook her head as she listened to Sara. "I was running the bathtub, . . . lots of noise. Didn't hear anything." She tapped her ear and looked apologetic. "Who would break in here anyway?"

Say again.

Who would break in? Why? she signed. "You're not thinking it was the can opener guy?"

Sara shrugged. "Who broke into Thurston

Court? Could have been anybody looking for cash, I guess. It's the holidays. Somebody might think we have a lot of spending money lying around."

Wouldn't that be nice, Keesha replied and went back to toweling her hair.

Sara walked to the window. The sun had fallen behind the mountain, and the old-fashioned street lamps had snapped on. Picture postcard material. She rubbed her eyes. Why couldn't she just relax like everybody else? Why couldn't she find logic in what she'd seen the way Bret had, the way Keesha did? What was in her that always searched out the irrational? She was Lieutenant Paul Howell's daughter, but Steve was his son. Steve was a cop, for that matter, yet he didn't let flashlight beams in the woods and half open utility room doors send his heart into overdrive.

She scanned the parking lot until she found the sports car she'd seen Chris Wheeler drive. She turned back to Keesha.

"That Wheeler guy could have pretended he needed the can opener so he could get in and look around."

"Case the joint?" Keesha laughed. "These are condominiums, Sara. Each unit is nearly identical to every other one. He wouldn't need to see it first. Neither would we. We could break into his unit or Damon and Bret's and know where everything was." She tapped her temple to ask if Sara understood.

"You made your point," Sara replied sourly. She looked back out the bedroom window until a tap on her shoulder made her turn around.

Keesha's deep brown eyes were wide with concern. "You're still on edge from all the mess in Radley. Nothing bad has happened here. It's New Year's Eve. We're all going to have a great time. Before you know it we'll be back in dull old Radley getting ready to go back to school." She tapped the windowpane. "It's magic out there. We'll all be together. Don't worry."

Sara sighed. *You know me better than I know myself.*

Marisa circled her open hand around her face then drew her fingers together at her chin, the sign for *beautiful*.

Sara's necklace gleamed over her ribbed shirt, and she fastened Keesha's neck piece over a simple silk blouse.

The three of them teased and complimented Steve when he finally came down from his second-floor room in the required jacket and tie. All four of them wore the glow of solid exercise and they were ready to party.

If Steve had any twinges of curiosity or doubts about Sara's observations, he'd decided not to mention it. There hadn't been a word about sugar houses or can openers.

Sara paused as she climbed the steps to the second level, the main entrance into the Spruce Ridge Inn. Memorabilia was everywhere. As Sara hung up her jacket she looked at the collection of sepia-colored photographs on the wall. There were four of sugar houses. Men and women in lumberjack shirts stirred kettles over open fires. Trees were full of spigots. Workhorses and their wagons stood ready.

Bret pointed to them. *See? I'll bet they've been using the sugar houses as long as that logging road's been here.*

Chapter 17

Sara hadn't counted on the response her necklace would get. So many people glanced at it — and her — that it felt like she was back at the museum with armed guards in every corner. Discomfort from the constant scrutiny crept across her shoulder blades.

It was odd and unsettling. Worse, it was affecting Bret.

What gives this time?

Sara shrugged.

I know you, Sara.

Okay, it's not the sugar house or any of that, I promise. I feel like everybody — or somebody — is looking at me.

Some are. You're beautiful tonight.

Thanks, that's not what I meant.

Bret sighed. *Don't make too much out of too little and please don't let it wreck tonight. We only have one more day.*

One more day was about all she could take, she wanted to say, but it wouldn't be fair. Besides, there were more unanswered questions in Radley than there were here. Bret was absolutely right. Her irrational sense of danger and doom would ruin the night for everybody if she let it.

In the course of the night Sara and Keesha's jewelry was always the focal point, but since the Eldridge Collection hadn't opened to the public till the day before no one knew the significance of what they were wearing. Keesha enjoyed showing off her Egyptian replicas, telling where they'd come from. After a dozen explanations, with many kids having trouble with her speech, Sara grew tired of it.

It was nearly ten P.M. and dessert was finished. Damon and Keesha announced that they were going skating and would meet Bret and Sara outside at the bonfire where the four of them could watch the spectacle on the slopes and the midnight fireworks.

Sara watched the couple disappear through the crowd and put her hand to her throat for the thousandth time. *I know it's because of the fund-raiser where they were watching everybody constantly, but I can't shake the feeling that when I wear this stuff the Radley Museum secret service is watching every move I make.*

Bret shook his head. *No secret service. It's just spectacular stuff, that's all. It stands out. You stand out. People are interested.*

Maybe so, but it gives me the creeps. Wearing this makes me feel like I have to watch everybody in the room . . . like something else is going to happen. Suddenly, she tapped her temple to indicate that she had an idea. Before Bret could protest, she tugged him up from his chair. They snaked their way through partying kids and up the stairs to find Steve and Marisa.

Sara motioned for Steve to be quiet as she came up behind Marisa and slipped the necklace around her neck.

Marisa's hands flew to her throat. "What's this all about?"

Sara went around to face her so she could read her lips. "It looks better on you tonight."

"Are you sure?"

Sara nodded.

Marisa patted the coins and smiled. "Thank you so much! I'll take good care of it. You don't need to worry about a thing, I've got my own undercover detective with me."

Much better, Sara signed to Bret once they were back at their table. She stretched her empty neck and laughed. *The weight of the world — gone!*

Bret frowned and bent close to the table-cloth as Sara signed. He picked up a large blue chip. "A gemstone fell out of your bracelet."

Sara put it in her palm and pushed it around with her index finger. "Super Glue. I'll glue it when we get back to Radley." She drummed the fingers of her free hand on the table. "This is just the excuse I need to put the bracelet away, too. I've been complaining, but I really do want these to last. The bracelet might lose more stones." She stood up. "Be right back. I'm going to put it in my jacket pocket. It'll be safe in there and I won't have to worry about any other stones falling out."

Sara leaned down and kissed Bret before she crossed the room one more time. She hurried to the stairs and went down to the coat room. She pointed to her parka and asked the woman in charge to help her as she zipped the bracelet and loose gemstone into an inner pocket.

Sara headed back to the party. She was alone on the stairs when she was grabbed by the shoulders from behind. Before she knew what had happened she was spun around and pushed against the railing. Someone in a blur of dark parka and ski mask grabbed her forearm and yanked her forward. "Where are they?"

His mouth was nearly obliterated by the mask. She yanked her hand back.

He repeated it, but before she could say anything, explain that she was deaf, or make sense of it, a couple came down the stairs. The man let go and ran. She watched as he pushed his way through the exit doors into the dark.

Chapter 18

She took the rest of the stairs two at a time and reached Bret nearly out of breath.

He jumped to his feet in alarm as she signed.

I was right! Some man grabbed me on the stairs. She put her hand around her forearm. *I knew it. Someone's been following us. I know it seems crazy, but whoever it was nearly knocked me off the stairs.*

Bret put his hand on her shoulders until she sat down, then signed back to her. *Slow down and explain.*

She did, but the minute she finished, Bret nudged her to look out the window. Outside on the deck the ski patrol was gathering to get ready to sweep the slopes. Every one was dressed in dark parkas and ski masks. *While you were downstairs the ski patrol came through. They announced that the sweep of the slopes will begin in a few minutes. Take a look. They're all dressed like the guy you described. What did he say to you?*

He said, "Where are they? Where are they?"

Bret looked skeptical. *Sara, even the best of us misread speech. You could read his lips that well through a ski mask?*

Yes!

Tell me what I'm saying. Bret dropped his hands and spoke while Sara watched with mounting irritation. He repeated himself.

She spoke in return. "You said, 'Where are they, where are they, where are they' just the way that guy did."

Bret shook his head. "The first time I said, 'Where are they.' The second time I said, 'Get out of my way.' The third one was 'You're in my way.'"

Angrily Sara signed *I know the difference between TH and W! I know what I saw!*

Of course you do. But why didn't he stay with you or take you outside where nobody could witness anything? You were right at the exit. It makes more sense that you bumped into one of the ski patrol in a hurry to get outside. Why don't we go up and tell Steve just to make sure.

Just to make me feel better? Sara turned her back and left for the loft before Bret could answer. Bret caught up with her as she found Steve and Marisa at their table. The minute she explained what had happened, she anticipated Steve's usual concern, but even he stayed relaxed.

"Three of the ski patrol members were just up here. They had their masks in their hands, but they were just the way you described," Marisa said.

"Why? Why were they up here?"

"To announce that they were about to sweep the slopes. To tell us to come and watch the ceremony and get ready for the fireworks."

Despite her frustration, Sara's face burned.

Steve patted her arm. "What about Keesha? Did anyone bother her?"

Sara yanked her thumb toward the window. "She's skating with Damon."

"If it'll make you feel better, I'll ask the manager if anyone's reported any problems. It's New Year's Eve. Thieves do crash parties like this — in and out with as many purses and wallets as they can grab. Maybe it was a pickpocket. When he saw that you didn't have your purse on your arm, he asked where it was, but then kept going. That's how they operate. Speed is everything. Hit and run . . . on to the next guy. Don't let this spoil your night with Bret," he added.

She sighed and looked at her date. "That's just what he said."

Sara and Bret met Keesha and Damon at the bonfire, but after Sara explained what had happened, Keesha also shook her head. "No one has bothered me."

Rather than get into more of a disagreement, Sara sighed and took Bret's arm as they crossed the snowy path that led back to the deck of the inn. Out above them the flames of the torches flickered as the ski patrol began their descent down Longview. The patterns of light were beautiful and she tried to get into the spirit of New Year's Eve.

Twenty minutes later from the top of the mountain the first sky rocket spread its fan of sparkling light. The sky erupted into a shower of illumination as the fireworks display began. Sara looked at Bret as his face was washed with the purple, then pink, then blue of the first set. She spotted Steve and Marisa not far from them, arms around each other's waists. It was a night for romance not fear, she told herself again, a night she didn't want to ruin for Steve, Bret, or Keesha. They'd all been through enough together already. She took one final deep breath and forced herself to join the sea of partygoers craning their necks to watch the display. All around her people cheered and clapped. She forced herself to join them.

At midnight when the last of the blasts had turned the sky a dozen shades of dazzling colors, Bret kissed her. She wrapped herself in his arms. Her heart hammered against him and even she couldn't tell if the hammering was from her love for Bret or the sense of foreboding that had seeped into her nearly a week earlier and was now bone-deep.

* * *

"Who wants to sleep in and who wants to ski tomorrow morning?" Steve asked as the group got off the shuttle bus at the condominiums.

Bret yawned and shoved his parka sleeve back to see his watch. "It's nearly one a.m. I vote for sleep."

"My last day. I vote for skiing. I'll sleep when we get back to Radley," Keesha said.

They finally agreed to meet at eleven for their last day on the slopes. After good-bye kisses and waves, the boys walked down the hill to their condominium. Keesha and Sara crossed the parking area to their front walk and came up behind Steve and Marisa who were already at the door.

At their condo the porch light was on and Sara watched Marisa chat with Steve as he worked the key in the lock. Suddenly Steve's expression changed. His eyebrows arched in shock. Keesha tried to rush forward, but he held her back. He turned to face them so there was no mistake. "Stay here." *Stay here.* He put his finger to his lips and shoved Marisa away from the door.

Chapter 19

Sara knew better than to question anything and stood frozen with the others. Steve
crouched and inched forward into the dark.
He pushed the door open with his boot. It
was then that she realized what had alarmed
her brother. Their front door had been ajar. It
must have given way as he put the key in the
lock.

He turned around one last time and gestured for them to stay where they were, then
eased himself through the doorway. He put
his arm out to the right and the foyer burst
into light as he hit the switch. Even from behind Steve, Sara could see that the skis that
had been propped against the banister had
fallen across the tile floor. He motioned them

to stay outside and moved across the room to the kitchen.

The place had been ransacked. Sara was hot, then suddenly cold. She huddled into her parka. Keesha grabbed her arm. From the porch they could see into the living room where drawers had been yanked open in the chest. Sofa pillows were ripped and strewn on the floor. The closet door was ajar and even the lid of the washing machine was open. Anger, fear, and disbelief shredded Sara's fatigue. Any thoughts of sleep evaporated.

An hour later Sara was still on the couch. The Spruce Ridge security patrol was first on the scene followed by the flashing blue lights of a Colby squad car. Sara, Keesha, and Marisa had done their best to put up with curious neighbors who had come by. Many were still arriving from the party at the inn, awake, inquisitive, then suddenly concerned about their own units.

Steve produced his Radley Police Department credentials to convince the authorities that they had no drugs in the condo that someone might be looking for, nothing of value except what they were wearing. All the cash they had was safe and sound in their wallets.

Sara wanted to talk to Steve but that would take time. At the moment he was at the dining table brushing his hand through his hair while he helped the authorities file a report.

"The poor guy does this for a living. Just when he gets a few days off, he has to go right back to police work," Sara said as Marisa sat down next to her.

"Thank goodness he's a cop. You couldn't hear how hard he had to work to convince these guys that there was nothing suspicious in the condo that someone might be after."

Keesha leaned over. "They said none of the other units was touched, just this one."

"So they try to turn it around and put the suspicion on us!" Sara's anger stiffened her shoulders. "Did Steve tell them about what happened to me at the inn?"

Marisa nodded and the three women exchanged glances. "You may have been right after all," Keesha finally said.

"Whoever was in the ski mask might not have been there to sweep the slopes," Sara said as clearly as possible.

"That's an understatement."

Sara looked from one concerned expression to the other. "What do we have that somebody wants? This doesn't make any sense. I hope Steve is also telling them about Chris Wheeler." She pushed herself up from the couch. "I need some air."

"Air? It two A.M." Marisa looked as though she hadn't understood.

Sara nodded. "A quick walk."

Keesha stood up, too. "I'll go with you."

Sara glanced once more at her brother. "Tell Steve so he doesn't panic."

Marisa nodded and tapped her watch. "Not too long. Take the flashlight."

"Just close by, maybe around to Logger's Run and back."

Once they were out under the street lamps, Sara looked down the hill at the sets of dark windows. "Why us? Everybody else goes back to sleep. Bret and Damon will be ready to ski tomorrow and we'll be zombies."

Keesha shrugged. "There's something about hanging around you that makes life exciting."

Sara threw up her hands. "Don't blame me for this."

"I don't blame anybody. I just wish I knew what they think we had that made it worth tearing the whole place apart."

As they left the glow of the street lamps, lipreading became difficult. Sara snapped on the flashlight and shone it between them, then touched Keesha's arm to get her to stop. "Was Chris Wheeler one of the neighbors who came by tonight?" She pantomimed a can opener to make sure Keesha understood.

Keesha paused, then shook her head. "I didn't see him, but remember, it's New Year's Eve. He's probably out with his girlfriend. Maybe they had better things to do than rubberneck at a break-in."

Sara frowned in confusion.

"No," Keesha reiterated. "Didn't see him."

They continued around the units to the back where Logger's Run led into the woods. Sara looked at her deck and the filtered light coming through the sliding glass doors in the living room. She could see Marisa at the dresser pushing the drawers back in.

"This is where he walked into the woods and over to the sugar house."

Sara and Keesha exchanged a glance. Sara leaned over and tucked her jeans into her boots. She shone the single beam of light ahead of them and watched it bounce off the trunks of the sugar maples until they found the opening that Wheeler had used as a path. Patches of moonlight sifted through the bare maples. After a night of chaos and surprise, the snowy silence was oddly comforting.

Keesha stopped abruptly and pulled the flashlight beam onto her face so Sara could read her lips. "Lucky you're deaf. You're used to silence. This is creepy."

"Want to go back?"

Keesha looked behind Sara as if to reassure herself that home was just yards away. "No. We've gone this far, let's see if we find anything."

By staying in Wheeler's path, little snow blocked their way. It was cold, however, and getting colder as they went deeper into the trees. The path took one right angle turn.

Keesha grabbed Sara's arm again. Ahead, barely visible in the snow, was an amber glow. The butter-colored circle faded to white then grays as if someone had lighted a votive candle in the snow.

At the same moment Sara and Keesha realized it was the glow of a dropped flashlight. Sara drew the beam of her own light over the area. Thick, bare trunks and spindly pine bows flashed in and out of focus. Suddenly Keesha pushed her arm sharply to the right until her flashlight picked up the shadow in a section of fresh powder. Chris Wheeler lay sprawled on his back, arms out like a snow angel. Sara put her free hand over her mouth and almost dropped the flashlight. The beam found his face. It was gray and his open eyes stared up into the bare branches of the sugar maple.

Chapter 20

Sara knelt in the snow and turned her beam on Keesha. "He's dead."

Keesha nodded. "Sara, I'm very frightened." She fanned the air. "Can you smell the whiskey? Drunk? Do you think he got drunk and stumbled over here by himself?"

The light on Keesha shimmered as she spoke and Sara realized her hand was shaking as she tried to keep the beam on her friend. Sara jumped to her feet, unable to read Keesha's lips. "This is the second body we've found this week. What's going on?"

Sara didn't care whether Keesha understood her or not. She stumbled to her feet and gritted her teeth against the sob caught in her throat.

* * *

She found Steve standing in the middle of the living room with two uniformed officers and the security representative from the lodge. He turned as she burst through the front door. She was tired of being brave, tired from the long night. Without a word she ran across the room and threw her arms around her brother's neck, crying loudly. It was Keesha who finally explained what had happened.

No one felt like skiing. No one felt like doing anything. "At least the police were already here when we found the body," Keesha said grimly. "Not that anybody could have saved him."

She and Sara were at the table picking at muffins and fruit. Now the view through the sliding glass doors included yellow crime scene tape wrapped around trees and across the path to the sugar house.

It had begun to snow as Bret and Damon arrived. They sat across the table with Marisa. Steve was, again, on the phone with the Colby Police Department.

"Do they still think it was hypothermia?" Bret asked as Steve put down the phone.

Steve nodded. "He was drunk. The paramedics think he passed out in the snow."

"In that cold, with no one to find him, it wouldn't take long. We see a few cases every year at the hospital, especially hunters," Marisa added.

"There was no identification on him. If it hadn't been for you girls, he'd still be out there."

"And maybe he wouldn't be found until someone decided to make maple syrup," Sara added once she'd read her brother's lips. *Maybe that's the way somebody wanted it.*

Bret arched his eyebrows at her comment and interpreted for Damon and Marisa.

"The name Christopher Wheeler isn't turning up a thing in Milton," Steve added. "Might be an alias; might be just what it appears."

"*Some guy stupid about alcohol?*" Sara shook her head. "*Why the sugar house again? Why was he out there in the dark, so late? Even if he doesn't have a record, I still think he's the one who broke in here. The can opener was an excuse. He's been hanging around us, watching this place. I'm sure the police will find the ski mask and parka someplace stupid like under his bed."*

Bret looked at Steve. "You said the police didn't find a thing from here on him, at the sugar house or in his condo. Nothing to indicate a robbery," he added as he spoke slowly to Sara.

"And nothing was missing here," Keesha said.

"Did he really see our lights on when he came over that first night or was he waiting for us? What did he think he'd find in here? Steve, couldn't this have something to do with a case of yours? Something from Radley?"

Without waiting for a reply Sara put her head down on her arms as she fought her exhaustion. It immediately cut her out of the conversation because she couldn't see anyone's speech. She didn't care. Sleep had consisted of a few hours of tossing and turning. She wasn't sure Steve had ever gone to bed.

Suddenly she stood up. "I tell you one thing. I'm not going to let this mess wreck the one day I have left. I don't know what's going on and right now I don't want to know. I'm going back to bed till two." She held up two fingers and tapped her watch. "Then I'm going skiing. This is the last chance we'll have."

Thursday morning in the Thurston Court apartment, Sara pulled breakfast together while Steve walked Tuck. Radley was gleaming under a fresh snowfall, the kind that covers bodies, she thought morosely.

Sara and Steve had unpacked and sorted out the laundry. Marisa was back at work. They had all given statements to the Colby police and left information about where they could be reached. Sara knew that Steve had also given information about what Radley cases he was involved with on the chance that a connection could be made between the break-ins.

The news in the *Gazette* included a small story on the funeral for Thomas Maloney, held the day before. While we took our final runs down Jackknife and Longview, Sara thought glumly.

She and Steve had examined the lock to their door. The Fletchers had already had the locks changed along with theirs, but scratches and dents were still evident in the woodwork where someone had used a pry tool of some sort. Thank goodness for Tuck. Sara gave him an extra hug when he came bounding in with her brother.

Over fruit salad and bagels, Steve broke the news that he'd already been called back to the station on a new case. "It may be long hours. Two of the guys are out on vacation this week."

Undercover?

Yes.

"*Will I be able to get in touch with you?*"

I don't know yet. I will try to call and let you know. Stay over at Keesha's tonight if you're uncomfortable.

I'm used to it. I'm fine, she signed back — mostly because she didn't want Steve to be out on the street in a dangerous situation worrying about whether or not his sister was comfortable home alone in their apartment.

Steve tapped her forehead. "*What is it then? What's bothering you . . . everything?*"

She gave him a thin smile and congratulated him on getting the ASL correct. "All these loose ends. When you go to the station, see what's new on the gun we found at the museum."

"It doesn't involve you."

"Please. One thing I haven't told you. . . . " She ran her fingers along her jaw. "Wheeler had shaved off a beard. Did you notice the tan line?"

"Sara —" A flush crept across Steve's cheeks.

"You noticed, too! I thought so! You're a great cop, Steve, you just won't give me any details. Shaving the beard could mean Wheeler was trying to change his appearance." *Change the way he looked.* "I thought he looked familiar —"

Steve grabbed her arm. "You recognized him?"

Sara shook her head. "No. No, I wasn't that sure. But I did ask him if he was from Radley. Remember? I told the police he said he was from Milton, not from around here. Will we ever know the truth?"

Steve shrugged. "We're all fine. We're not

missing anything. Everybody's healthy. I'll leave finding the truth to the Colby police." He tapped his temple.

Yes, she'd understood.

When they'd finished eating, Sara tapped Steve for one more question. "Super Glue? I want to fix my bracelet."

Steve shook his head. "Don't use glue. It will discolor the gold."

She frowned in confusion. *Say again.*

Won't work well. He dropped his hands, unsure about the sign. "The bracelet's too nice. Take it up to Wagner Jewelers and have them reset the stone." He scribbled out the name and address on a piece of paper. "Dad used Charles Wagner for years." He pulled his key chain from his pocket. "It's the place where we got this for Dad that Christmas. Won't be expensive and it shouldn't take long."

Steve left for the station in his usual ratty jeans and sweatshirt, a clean set of more normal clothes in his duffel. Sometimes he told her what his assignment was and sometimes he couldn't. She learned long ago that there was no sense in worrying over what she couldn't change.

As she crossed the kitchen, the blinking light told her someone was at the door. She waited and watched for the blinking to turn to a pattern of short and long flashes. She grinned and pressed the buzzer. Bret was in the lobby.

When she opened the door, he leaned over to ruffle Tuck's fur then kissed her warmly. *I came over to take you to the museum so I can get my own private tour of the collection.*

Sara laughed. *Won't be very private. Might be really crowded. I don't know if I want to go back. So much has gone on this week and it all started over there with that poor guard.*

Bret tried to be flippant. *Look at it this way. You've already found two bodies. What more can happen?*

Chapter 21

How about that old superstition that things always happen in threes?

Bret began to tick things off on his fingers. "Dead guard. Gun. Dead guy in the snow. Ransacked condo. Attempted break-in here." *I think you went over your limit.*

In other words, stop worrying.

Exactly. Let's try to enjoy ourselves. We can skate later, after they clear the rink.

Sara nodded, glad for the diversion. She settled Tuck and put away the last of the dishes. At the last minute she grabbed the flannel bag with her bracelet. As they left the apartment she explained her errand, glad that Bret knew where Wagner Jewelers was located.

* * *

The first thing Sara pointed out to Bret wasn't anything in the Eldridge Collection, it was the employees' parking lot where she'd found Thomas Maloney. *Keesha and I ran up here to the parking attendant to get help — not that it made any difference. The gun was over there.* She shivered as Bret looked up at the roof. Wind spun the new snow into drifts against the building.

Bret put his arm around her. *If anybody suspects a thing about this guy's death, you know Steve will hear about it at the station.*

He said he'd try to find out if there's anything on the gun or the death, she added. She hoped there wasn't and had to admit she didn't have any reason beyond her emotions to suspect anything.

They walked half a block to the entrance to the Hall of Architecture. Anxiety began to work its way into her stomach. She should never have started the tour by showing Bret where she'd found the guard. She was flooded with dread. It had been Maloney's gun; she'd known it all along. She intended to press Steve to find out if the butt end of the handle showed any marks as if he'd used it to hammer. It was loaded and she knew as well as her brother the idea was preposterous. Who had he been aiming at? Why?

Everything she'd been trying to forget flooded over her as she climbed the Grand Staircase. She explained how the gates had been drawn across the staircase during her sneak preview and the trouble she thought she'd caused. Trouble that never left.

The exhibit was busy, but not as crowded as she'd assumed.

Sara tugged Bret by the wrist, around a group of people, to the back wall of the Gothic cathedral. She pointed to the back stairs. *Look at that cat. I came up the stairs and it scared me to death. I don't know why, it just stares out into space. Actually, that afternoon it was staring out at the security guard. Nothing has been right since, now that I think about it.*

Same one?

She shook her head and finger spelled. *D-A-V-I-D C-A-L-D-W-E-L-L. He works here and was in charge of the party.*

Did he give you the jewelry?

Sara shook her head. *Wrong again. That guy was here from M-I-A-M-I with E-L-D-R-I-D-G-E.* Her fingers flew as she finger-spelled the names for which she had no sign. *C-A-L-D-W-E-L-L is the one who called Keesha's mom to see if we were okay after he heard we found the body. He was nervous about making everything perfect.* She snapped her fingers. *You saw him. And I noticed him outside the apartment when we were walking Tuck in the snow. I ran into him again with Keesha at the Side Door.*

Sounds like he was following you.

He might have been. The afternoon I came up here, he was over there by the mural, then he just disappeared.

Bret walked with her across to the painting, the first time she'd been closer than twenty feet. He ran his hand over a door, cut flush with the wall, without any frame or jamb. The Egyptian scenes continued right over it. Even the hinges and small doorknob were camouflaged by being set into the action of the mural. *Employees' door. They're*

*designed for staff to get from one place to an-
other in a hurry, or storage, or security.
Mansions have them for servants.*

Amazing! I didn't even notice it till now,
Sara replied.

That's probably the point. Look at this.
Bret touched the knob and the door inched
open. A thin rectangle of duct tape had been
pressed over the lock. *The only reason you
did notice it was because it's broken.*

*It must go somewhere because I saw
C-A-L-D-W-E-L-L and R-I-L-E-Y here, C,
GUARD, and S, JEWELRY,* Sara signed.
*Name signs for them so I can stop finger
spelling. Maybe there's a shortcut for staff
down to the offices or into the security center.*

Curiosity got the better of her and she
inched around Bret so she could see. Just inside the door to the right, directly behind the
mural wall were the wheeled storage carts
that held round tables. On the left, in an open
alcove behind the Sphinx, stacks of gilded
chairs were lined up against the wall. She
came back out and Bret shut the door.

*These were all used for the party last Sat-
urday,* she signed.

And nobody had to carry them very far, he replied.

It's like a tunnel into the guts of the museum, Sara signed.

Bret shook his head at her. *Kill your curiosity. Tell me about Caldwell.*

Sara nodded as they left the mural. *He was there with Riley when I snuck up here. He worried that I had overheard security plans, but had no idea I was deaf. He wanted everything perfect for Saturday. He's the guy I saw on the sidewalk. He followed me to tell me not to discuss anything. That's when he realized I hadn't heard a thing.*

Bret hugged her. *I'm sorry this is still upsetting you.*

They signed as they walked and entered the Egyptian Room after Bret saluted the Sphinx. It was crowded, but people were moving. By the time they finished looking at the museum's sarcophagus and reconstructed tomb, the display cases were free.

All this stuff is priceless? Bret signed.

Pretty much. Read the cards. E-L-D-R-I-D-G-E has been collecting bits and pieces for thirty years.

Bret nodded as he read the information on the small cards. He tapped the case that displayed the original of Keesha's neck piece. *It looks identical. So do the bracelets. Why does he have copies of everything?*

His assistants said they're used for educational programs: for school visits, lectures, fund-raisers like the one here. That kind of thing.

Eldridge must be quite a guy.

When they'd finished in the Egyptian Room, they crossed the foyer to the Greek Room.

When they reached the display case that held the serpent bracelet, Sara leaned over and tapped the case. The original lay on indigo velvet, with the real gems gleaming in its eyes and down its back. Her wrist tingled. It felt odd to have spent so much time with the copy wrapped around her forearm.

Sara tried to get caught up in Bret's enthusiasm, but every blank stare of every statue made her stomach knot. One minute her head filled with the image of Thomas Maloney dead and alone in the parking lot under a dusting of snow. The next moment Chris Wheeler's unfocused stare was taking its place.

She glanced around. No alarms were going off. No one was going to grab her on a dark staircase and surely no more dead bodies were going to show up in her path. Nevertheless she stayed on edge. Whatever was making her feel this way nagged at her.

Sara leaned against a Corinthian column while Bret looked at the last case, a collection of gold pocket watches. As he bent over for a closer look, his posture pinched her memory. Something, someone, someplace similar? Where had she seen Bret bend in just that way before? What had he been looking at the first time? The first time . . . the first time. . . . She lost it as he finished and walked over to her.

You okay? He signed.

Yes. When you looked at those watches, you reminded me of something I can't quite place. It was like I'd seen you do it before. How could she explain that she'd be fine once they left the museum, once the plaster, marble, and granite eyes of Sphinxes, goddesses, and gargoyles weren't following her over every inch of the exhibit? She snuggled into the crook of his arm as they made their way back through the room into the foyer.

Can you show me where you took the art classes?

Downstairs. She walked with him back to the cathedral facade. This time as they reached the banister cat, Bret squatted down level with its stare. He looked across at the niche behind the Sphinx then stood up and laughed. *It really does look as though he's staring at something. Probably an Egyptian mouse over there behind the Sphinx.*

Sara smiled but anxiety overwhelmed her as they went down the narrow staircase. At the spot where Thomas Maloney had angrily asked her what she was doing, she paused. Bret simply nodded in understanding.

Once they left the stairs, she hurried along the corridor until Bret finally asked her to slow down.

She circled her heart: *Sorry.* At that moment a group of grammar school kids filed from the classroom, each carrying a piece of sculpture.

She showed him where the security offices were and the meeting room where they'd planned the gala.

I feel like I'm in a spy movie down here with all these special rooms and passageways.

With Bret in tow she wound her way through the labyrinth that made up the lower level of the Radley museum complex then back to the enclosed staircase and up to the Hall of Architecture.

Had enough? Sara signed.

Bret nodded. *You're the one who looks ready to leave. I wish you could shake this thing that's bothering you.*

So do I. Nothing? Something? I never thought it would bother me to come back.

But it did.

Don't get angry all over again. It's just a feeling, whenever I go in there, that something's not right. She shrugged it off with a tap on her purse. *Let's get to the jewelers, then a cafe — someplace that has nothing to do with the museum.*

They left for the car as she jangled the serpent bracelet in her hand.

Chapter 22

They pulled into the small parking area behind Wagner Jewelers as a plow left, and congratulated themselves on finding an open space. The wind was up, but the snow had stopped and patches of sunlight streamed through the clouds.

The only other customer left as the two of them approached the counter. Sara pulled the bracelet from her bag and laid it on the glass top along with the loose stone. Slowly and as clearly as possible she explained who she was.

Charles Wagner smiled. "I remember you and your brother a few Christmases ago. Something for your father . . . cuff links?"

Sara looked at Bret who repeated it in ASL. *Cuff links.*

"No, it was a key chain. Steve still uses it."

"Good. A tragedy, losing your father that way." He turned to study the loose stone she'd pulled from her purse.

Sara picked up the bracelet. "I was going to glue it, but I can see there were prongs for the gemstone. Steve says glue might ruin the gold or whatever it is."

The jeweler nodded. He examined it with his eyepiece, then looked at Sara. His searching expression moved to Bret. He signaled that he would be in the back room. Sara could glimpse brighter light and the elbow of someone at the workbench.

She was about to ask Bret what was going on when he bent over the counter as he had at the museum display case. Again the vague recollection teased her memory. Where had she seen Bret do that? The answer came to her with such force she jumped back against the counter. Bret turned in alarm as she cried out.

"Sara?"

"I remember!" *When you leaned over the watch display . . . oh Bret, it wasn't you I'd seen before — it was W-H-E-E-L-E-R.*

From skiing?

He shaved his beard, but I think I saw him in the museum during that last rehearsal. He was with Riley looking at the display case in the Greek Room. He was here! Bret! What is going on?

She was interrupted by the return of Charles Wagner and the jeweler from the back room. He laid the bracelet and stone on the jeweler's tray and looked up sharply at Sara. "You're certainly right not to glue this. It isn't a gemstone, it's a sapphire. Is this a family piece?"

Sara looked at Bret, sure she'd misunderstood.

He says it's a real stone. Sapphire.

"I hope someone explained to you what a valuable piece it is." He shook his head vehemently. "No glue."

"I know it's a good copy of a princess's bracelet."

He turned it over in his hands. "It's obviously an antique of some sort. Ruby, emerald, and sapphires here. . . . " He poked the design. "Look at the wear along the inside. This is nearly pure gold. Not very satisfactory for jewelry, but valuable."

Sara's speech faltered as she tried to explain. Neither man spoke. They exchanged a glance which settled along her spine. "What is it? You don't believe me?" Sara put her hands on the counter. "I have more at home. Can you look at them right now?"

Bret repeated what she'd asked and barely waited for the jewelers' nods before they charged through the doors for the car.

Sara sat up on Bret's passenger seat and signed as he started the ignition. *If I'm right about W-H-E-E-L-E-R, it makes everything else make sense. He was in the museum during rehearsals. That means he would have been trusted by the men in charge of the collection. Maybe he had access to it. Maybe he found out Keesha and I were going to be given the stuff as keepsakes. He saw his chance. Don't you see, Bret? He switched the jewelry so he could steal it from us later. If he ransacked our apartments and stole — I don't know — TV sets, other jewelry, it would never look like he was just after the museum stuff. E-L-D-R-I-D-G-E wouldn't know and no one at the museum would care because they all think the real stuff is all locked up in the displays, safe and sound.*

Bret's complexion had paled and his mouth was a thin, grim line. *For once, I think you're on to something. He could have been the guy who grabbed you New Year's Eve, dressed like the patrol so no one would suspect. He was probably desperate at that point because every time he broke in to grab the stuff, it was missing. Maybe he was going to hide it at the sugar house until you left.*

Until he got drunk from frustration and died of hypothermia first, Sara added.

They looked at each other for one long moment until Bret pulled her into his arms. She held on for dear life, aware, at last, of how close she'd been to real danger since the night of the glittering fund-raiser.

Once they had driven back to Thurston Court for the rest of the jewelry, and entered the Howell apartment, Sara called the Fourth Precinct police station on her TTY. Steve needed to know what she suspected. She could leave it to him to contact the Colby police. He'd left the apartment dressed for undercover work, and it was no surprise that he was unavailable. Since Wheeler was no longer a threat, Sara decided the information could wait until Steve came off his shift. Exhausted or not, she could tell him in person. She hung up relieved that none of it had anything to do with her brother or his police work.

Sara grabbed a brown paper sandwich bag from the kitchen and the coin necklace from her bedroom. Tuck had followed her from room to room, tail wagging in anticipation. "Later," she said as she patted him. "When I get back, we'll take a nice long walk and I'll tell you all about this."

Bret was already across the hall at the Fletchers' door. *No answer,* he signed as Sara appeared in her doorway. The Fletchers had been her second family since the death of her mother and Sara had often used the spare key to their apartment, knowing they wouldn't object if she let herself in. As she had hoped, Keesha's neck piece and scarab bracelets were on the dressing table in her bedroom.

Sara handed them to Bret and tore a piece of notebook paper from her best friend's school binder.

Keesha,
After the jeweler fixed my bracelet, he wanted to see all the pieces. I have yours, too. Will explain tonight. Will call when I get back.

Sara

She left the note in plain sight inside the front door. The Fletchers had been through enough and she wanted to alert them immediately that she had been inside.

It was nearly four P.M. by the time Bret drove her back to Wagner Jewelers. Charles Wagner was busy with a customer, but the minute he finished he motioned them to the counter. He put down two jeweler's trays and Sara laid the Egyptian neck piece in one and the scarab bracelets and her necklace in the other.

"There's been a terrible mistake," she said slowly. "These are supposed to be copies from the museum, from the Eldridge Collection." Sara expected the jeweler to frown in confusion, as she tried to explain the complicated story. Instead, Charles Wagner's stare was steady. He nodded and motioned for his assistant.

"This is Howard Baum, our expert in antique master craftsmanship."

Baum shook her hand, then Bret's. "I went to the exhibit Sunday. Frankly, if Charles hadn't assured me that you were Paul Howell's daughter, I would have called the police before you left the shop."

Sara's eyes widened in surprise. "We did call. Steve will take care of everything tonight. It's complicated, but you don't need to worry." She stopped as the men bent over the jewelry, then lifted the necklaces to the light.

Howard Baum shook his head and laid Keesha's neck piece back on the tray. "Copy. The beadwork is glass, excellently done, but the work is strung on some sort of plastic thread. Fishing wire?" He smiled to himself.

Charles Wagner put his hand up in warning. "Not here. These are the real thing." He showed them the delicate handwork on the gold wire links between the scarabs of Kee-sha's bracelets. He removed his eyepiece. "So is your necklace. These are authentic Greek coins."

". . . that the Prince of Mulvaria had fash-ioned into the necklace for his bride," Bret finished for him. "I just read the card in the display case this afternoon at the museum."

"And that's where we're going," Sara added. She turned to Bret. *Would you explain that because I was part of the fund-raiser, I know exactly who to return them to? We can get them right over to the museum before the security office closes.*

As Bret interpreted for her, she took a deep breath. What she didn't want to explain was the nagging fear that somebody beside Chris Wheeler might have been part of the plan, somebody like Sean Riley whom she'd seen with Wheeler. She needed to go directly to David Caldwell. With any luck at all, she could return everything. He could place the originals in the cases and R.C. Eldridge would never know.

Chapter 23

Wagner slid the jewelry carefully into padded boxes. "Let me call the museum police. I'm sure they'll send a car right over. This is much too valuable for you to be —"

"No!" Sara forced herself to relax. "That is, no thank you. Bret can drive right there. It's only a few blocks and I know just where to go. I want to keep this quiet until it's back in the right hands. If you called it would involve too much explaining, too many people. I know exactly where to return it."

Bret looked at his watch. ". . . And it's almost five o'clock, museum closing time."

After another round of thanks, Sara put the boxed jewelry into the paper bag and folded the sack carefully into her large shoulder bag.

With one last good-bye, she followed Bret to the parking lot.

They parked in the main museum lot like normal art patrons and got out of the car. Sara hesitated as they waited for departing traffic to pass. She was mentally exhausted, tense and in no mood to worry about whether Bret could understand her speech. Instead she shoved her gloves in her pockets and kept her shoulder bag safely tucked against her ribs as she spoke with her hands. *The shortest way to the security offices is in the back through the employees' entrance, but somebody will stop us and ask what we're doing. Follow me again around to the front. Do you still have our ticket stubs?*

Bret pulled them from his pocket.

They hurried side by side down the snow-lined sidewalk. Bret's expression told Sara he was as anxious to be rid of the jewelry as she was. If only it were as easy to give back the week's worth of anguish and tragedy.

For the second time that day they entered the building and showed their tickets. The woman at the desk waved them through with a reminder that the exhibit would close in twenty minutes. They sidestepped a Scout leader as she herded a Brownie troop down the Grand Staircase and into the gift shop.

This is our last chance, Sara signed, and pointed to the display cases.

Bret crossed the foyer for the Greek Room as if he'd read her mind. Less than a dozen people were in the wing, none of them paying any attention to them. *I can't tell the difference even now,* he said as Sara pulled the repaired bracelet from its box.

She opened the lid on the necklace case and compared, copy to original, copy to original. She shook her head. The shock had worn off, but the reality of how casually she'd treated the gold and ivory made her hands clammy. The entire design was connected with two-hundred-year-old gold links and she'd nearly thrown it around Marisa's neck New Year's Eve! She'd stuffed the bracelet into her parka pocket as if it were a used candy wrapper.

What is it? Bret signed.

She put everything back in her purse. *Let's*

get this stuff back to Caldwell before I do any more damage.

They went back through the portals, past the Greek statuary keeping eternal guard. Once out in the foyer she looked at Bret as he glanced up at the Sphinxes. *One last look at Keesha's jewelry, too?*

He shook his head. *I want to get this stuff back where it belongs and get out of here. Look at those Sphinxes, half smiling like they knew all along what a fiasco you got yourself into.*

It's too late for jokes. Two people are dead, Bret, and somebody Caldwell and E-L-D-R-I-D-G-E trusted masterminded the whole thing, right under their noses.

The art collector needs a name sign, too. E, MONEY, how's that?

They'd reached the internal staircase and Sara avoided the Egyptian cat. As Bret stared up at the cathedral facade, he crossed the columns and doors to look at the gargoyles. Motion made Sara turn. She looked back at the Sphinxes. Someone bumped her so hard that she fell on the marble floor and winced.

By the time Bret reached her, she was up

on one knee. He put his hand out and helped her up. *Did you slip?* he signed while she dusted herself off.

Somebody came out of nowhere. I don't know what his hurry was. Do they arrest you if you're thirty seconds late leaving the building?

They both turned in time to see the back of a man as he darted through the stragglers about to work their way down the Grand Staircase to the lobby. As Sara's head cleared, she clapped her hand over her mouth and stifled a cry.

What? Sara, what is it?

He stole my bag! Bret, it's gone. She looked frantically to both sides of her, grabbed Bret by the wrist, and ran for the entrance.

Chapter 24

*F*ace it, Sara, the bag is gone.

All around them the street swarmed with
five o'clock traffic, commuters, and pedestri-
ans. Most were huddled into scarves, hats,
and jackets, bundled against the weather. The
thief could have been standing at the curb
hailing a cab and she never would have recognized him.

Sara swiped angrily at the tears on her
cheeks as they came back into the Hall of Architecture. *This is a nightmare! My wallet,
all my identification, not to mention the jewels. That thief doesn't even know what he's
got.* Back inside at the desk she asked for
David Caldwell and explained that she knew

the way to his office. For the third time that afternoon, she and Bret climbed the Grand Staircase and crossed the marble foyer.

Why didn't we just walk right across here and down the back stairs half an hour ago? If I hadn't wanted to see the stupid copies —

Bret cupped her hands between his, then dropped them. *Stop blaming yourself. It's done. It's not your fault you had the stuff to begin with. You're lucky you weren't hurt.*

They rushed across the foyer and down the stairs, once more past the spot where she'd run into Maloney. Guns, bodies, now this. Bret squeezed her hand.

Sara hurried down the corridor to the room where David Caldwell had first displayed the leather box. Such excitement, she thought. Such a long time ago. She shut her eyes against the mental image of Chris Wheeler's blue-skinned stare into the Spruce Ridge sky. She'd linked him to Riley and sooner or later, whether it was Steve or the Colby police, she knew somebody would put the rest of the pieces together, pieces that joined them all to the priceless jewelry that had just been stolen from her.

At the far end of the hall a security gate had been pulled between where she stood and the entrance. Sara entered the open door of David Caldwell's office. At the same moment he seemed to fly at her. He had a cellular phone to his ear. She'd expected a look of surprise on his face, but he seemed almost smug.

"It is you! Security just called from the entrance. Someone snatched your bag while you were in the exhibit?" He handed her a form and poked the paper as if he didn't expect her to understand what he'd said. "Fill this out while I'm on the phone."

She looked at Bret, but the expression on his face sent chills down her arms.

I'm deaf, Bret signed.

Say again.

He glanced sharply at Caldwell's back. *Don't give me away. I'm deaf.*

She nodded. Caldwell wandered out of sight and into his inner office with the phone.

Sara looked at Bret. *What is it?*

He's talking to somebody about us and the jewelry. He said, "Security caught her on camera in the Greek Room. She and this other deaf kid actually brought the stuff right into the exhibit. I know he's deaf, too. They've been using sign language. We made it look like a purse snatching. No sweat. She has no idea she's had the real stuff. It was so easy. That idiot W-H-E-E-L-E-R blew three days trying to get it. Took me two minutes. I'll bet he's turning over in his grave, if he's in one yet."

Sara's blood froze. *W-H-E-E-L-E-R!* W, *T-H-I-E-F,* a perfect name sign if there ever were one.

Bret pressed his index finger against her lips. *"Trust me on this one,"* he's saying now. *"Don't screw it up with your lousy orders from a thousand miles away, Eldridge wants it tonight."*

No! Are you sure that's who —

Bret's nod was adamant. *He's talking again. He's saying: "It's all set, I swear . . . without a hitch. I'll think of some explanation and get rid of them. We just closed. I've got the gates up till I'm finished. Five-thirty to six. The mayor's due in the lecture hall and I worked up a phony threat. Sent our regular guards over there to inspect every inch of the place."*

Bret arched his shoulders in question and motioned that Caldwell had stopped talking. *He's quiet. Listening?* Bret took up signing again. *He says: "This is no place to go into details. Not on the office phone. M-A-L-O-N-E-Y and W-H-E-E-L-E-R were the only ones who knew anything and I got rid of them."* He's saying, *"Trust me, S-E-A-N, R.C. thought we got the real stuff back days ago and now we finally do. Stone deaf, both of them. I'll send them home. Just me. The burglary'll take twenty minutes. It'll be taken care of just the way I promised. Just get over here and be ready to leave with the real stuff."*

Before she could make sense of what Bret had signed, Caldwell returned to the room. She scribbled her name and address on the form to give herself time to think. She wrote descriptions of the purse and its contents while her mind raced back to Bret's signing. If she'd understood him correctly, Eldridge

was authorizing Caldwell and his assistant
Sean Riley to burglarize his own collection.

Caldwell smiled ingratiatingly at both of
them as Sara handed him the form. "Thank
you. I'll fill out a report and file it with the
Radley police, too, since you saw the thief
leave the building. We'll call if we come up
with anything. Now follow me. I have to un-
lock the hall gate to let you out. We keep this
end of the building under tight security." As
he spoke he gestured with ridiculous hand
signals as if neither she nor Bret had a brain
in their heads.

None of that mattered. Out of the building
was exactly where she wanted to be, out and
on the TTY to Steve's precinct office. Let
Caldwell think she and Bret were too stupid
to understand what was about to happen. She
sucked in short, shallow breaths to slow her
heart. How could she have been so wrong
about him?

If Caldwell hadn't had her purse stolen she
and Bret would be spilling their guts right
this minute, telling the man who'd murdered

Maloney and Chris Wheeler how they discovered they had the real jewelry. She shivered even though she still wore her parka. Out. The sooner the better. She could get a police net to the Hall of Architecture before David Caldwell finished emptying the display cases.

As Sara stood up to leave, a man charged into the room nearly knocking into Bret. Sara's shoulder bag was in his hand and he looked suspiciously like the man who'd grabbed it. Even a hearing person could have read the look of shock on his face as he realized that Sara was still in the office.

Caldwell glared at him with an expression of pure hatred. "You fool!"

Play dumb, Sara signed to Bret.

Bret's eyes widened, but he stood still as she clapped her hands together. "You found my bag! Thank you. I'm deaf." She tapped her ears. "Can't hear a thing. Whoever took it snuck up behind me."

The man glanced from Sara to Caldwell and back. "Security. Parking lot. Found it by the gate." He handed it to her.

As calmly as she could, Sara made a production of checking the contents. The paper bag with the Wagner Jewelers boxes was gone. A ten dollar bill was missing from her wallet and her identification cards and library card were scattered inside. He'd done a good job of making it look like a real robbery, she thought. Play dumb, Sara, she demanded. Play dumb and save your life.

He knows. The guard's black-eyed stare seemed to bore into the middle of her skull as she glanced up from the bag. The jewelry boxes! He would have seen "Wagner Jewelers" printed on the boxes and known immediately that she'd been to a professional. He muttered something to Caldwell.

Whatever Bret heard, he didn't interpret. Instead he clamped his hand around Sara's wrist and yanked her with him into the hall.

Chapter 25

Her hip hurt where she'd been pushed to the floor but adrenaline pumped through every inch of her body. There was no time to try and make sense of Eldridge or Caldwell or the accomplice who'd grabbed her purse. Wheeler was dead. Maloney was dead. Whatever this fake burglary was all about, it was also about murder. Sara looked over her shoulder at the gate blocking the exit. The only other exit she knew of were the fire doors at the end of the classroom wing.

With Bret beside her she changed directions and tore forward to the classroom wing. She slammed to a halt as they rounded the bend. The long hall was dark, every door closed. At the far end EXIT shone in glowing red letters over the fire doors, but another gate had been pulled between the exit and where she stood.

Bret put his arm on her shoulder as they panted. *They're not following us! On the phone he was yelling about only having twenty minutes to pull this off. Sara, we're locked in here. He knows we can't go anywhere but upstairs to the exhibit where they'll be. I'm sure Caldwell's got all the cameras and sirens off while he pulls this job. Then he'll come back, turn on the cameras, and find us.*

She nodded numbly. *This must have been what he was planning when I saw him a few days ago. The guard who found me insisted that no one else had clearance. No one knew he was up there. When he found out I set off the alarm he thought I'd heard it all! No wonder he looked so relieved and shocked when I told him I was deaf.* She stopped as a figure came up behind her. Sara's scream stayed in her throat as Caldwell slammed his hand over her mouth.

"I don't care if you can read my lips and understand this or not. I don't have any more time to waste with you two." He nodded as the guard wrestled Bret's arms behind his back and swung a length of duct tape around his wrists. "No more sign language. No more acting stupid. I need a hostage and you're it. I've got less than half an hour to make this work. You go with Landers, here."

With a final nod, Caldwell dragged Sara in front of him and pushed her up the stairs to the Hall of Architecture. She could tell by the vibrations and knocking on the stairs that Bret and Landers were right behind her.

Just as abruptly, they stopped at the top. Caldwell nodded and Landers yanked another length of duct tape from the roll. This time he bound her wrists together behind her back in one swift motion. Until that moment she was more angry than frightened, but as Caldwell pulled Bret with him across the foyer toward the Greek Room, Landers pulled a bandanna from his jeans. At first she thought he was going to tie her to the banister — as if she had any place to run. But the anger turned to terror as he whipped the cotton across her eyes.

"No!" She was sure she screamed because

a hand slapped roughly over her mouth, then worked the fabric into a knot that dug into the back of her head. In that instant her world was reduced to a black chasm of terror. She couldn't hear and she couldn't see. She didn't dare cry out for Bret in case his reaction would give away the fact that his hearing was as sharp as his captors'. Instead she muffled her cry as she was pushed roughly backward and left.

Don't panic, don't panic, don't panic. The mental chant became a litany as she forced the terror down. Small breaths. Common sense. She made a mental image of where she stood. Behind her, she inched her hands up as far as they would go. Railing. Forward. Cat. The banister cat. She kept the image in her head. Concrete images. No panic. Small breaths. No panic but stone-cold fear.

She could only get one hand on the cat. She knew where she was, but where were they going to take Bret? And what would they do to him when they discovered he'd heard everything? Tears squeezed through her lashes and into the bandanna. She felt the cat, the spine, the head and those unblinking, eternally staring eyes. They became her eyes, staring across the room. The panel. As clearly as if she were looking, Sara saw the door in the Egyptian panel. She'd only glanced at it, but it was more than a storage room. It was a path to somewhere — anywhere would help.

Praying she was quiet, hoping Caldwell was still in the Greek Room, she put one foot in front of the other and walked directly ahead, straight across the empty marble floor, head forward, shoulders hunched, afraid of banging into the wall, yet desperate to reach it. It felt like five minutes but in more like twenty seconds her shoulder rubbed the base of the Sphinx.

She kept going. Finally, she came to the mural. Her pulse banged in her temples as she felt the door behind her. She bent until her hand brushed the knob.

In. She was in. She closed the door behind her. Without her sight the space shrank. She felt like Alice in Wonderland suddenly huge in a shrinking hall. She hunched again afraid of banging into walls, knocking over the tables or worse, somehow setting them rolling endlessly down the narrow pathway. They'd hear her. They'd kill Bret. They'd killed before.

She knocked into a stack of chairs. They were piled, seat on seat, and Sara tilted her head until she felt what she was after, the upright legs of a gilt chair. She prayed she was being quiet as she knelt down and scraped the chair leg against her head until it hit the bandanna. Up, then down again she inched and coaxed the blindfold up, over her forehead. Sight!

The space was wider than she'd thought, and long. Long enough to take her to another part of the complex, any place beyond the gates Caldwell had wrapped around his little corrupt world.

The narrow space was lit with small low watt bulbs, too low to illuminate what lay at the dark spot at the far end. She crept forward. She moved another ten feet. There was another door. It gave her something to focus on as she stumbled forward praying that she could pull it open and find herself safely somewhere — anywhere else.

The mental picture shattered as the passageway plunged into darkness. She was back in the chasm, disoriented. Someone had turned off the light. Someone was inside with her. Someone she couldn't hear. She pressed herself against the wall to keep her sense of direction. Then she shrank to the floor until she could press her bound hands on it. Motion; she could feel the tremble of footsteps. Someone was in here. Sara scrambled to her feet.

Whether it was Landers or Caldwell, they were both part of museum security. Either would know every nook of the building. She moved forward, gritting her teeth against the anticipation of smacking into the door. In another five steps she hit it full force and sank to her knees. Not an inch of light escaped from around the frame. What were the chances that she had wedged herself into a death trap? What were the chances that her body wouldn't be found until someone needed the tables for another fund-raiser months from now?

She landed on her knees and turned, fingers grasping, straining to reach the knob. It was slicker, smoother than the banister cat.

She slipped, unaware until then how sweaty her hands were. Sara stood up and pressed until her fingers reached firmly around the knob. It turned. She pulled. It opened. Light, dim as it was, beamed at her from below. She was at a stair landing. Her nostrils flared at the sharp smell of disinfectant. Clean. Well used. That meant the stairs went somewhere. People used the staircase. Janitors cleaned it. Bound hostages escaped by it.

She stumbled in the light and worked her way down the first two steps and then beams of light shot up into her face. She crooked her head and tried to shield herself from being blinded as she lost her balance. Somebody was at the bottom of the stairs; but as she tried to catch herself, hands shoved her from behind and she was pushed violently forward down the staircase.

Chapter 26

Sara fell. Someone yanked her up by the shoulders and threw her sideways. She turned as whoever it was raced past her, up the stairs and through the door. Her focus grew hazy. *They didn't want me after all,* she thought dimly as she slumped back down and tumbled over the remaining steps to the bottom.

She blinked and winced against the pain in her shoulder as someone hauled her to her feet. "Steve!" Like some vision from a magic act, her brother, still dressed in his jeans and sweatshirt, pulled her into a hug and helped her through one last doorway. She blinked against the glare of the overhead hall lights.

"I'll be back. Don't move."

Before she could respond, he had gone up the staircase. She was sitting on the other side of the gate still strung across the hallway. True to his word, Steve was back five minutes later.

He sliced the duct tape from her wrists with his pocket knife and she threw her arms around his neck. *How did you know? What are you doing here?*

He poked her shoulder. "You left a trail only a cop could follow. I got back to the station a little over an hour ago. There was a message from the Colby police." He tapped his temple. Sara nodded that she was following.

"They found a half burned fax in Wheeler's fireplace that mentioned the sugar house and warned him not to be stupid like Maloney. Unsigned, but enough to tie Wheeler to the museum. I remembered that you were going to the jeweler's. I called Wagner. He told me what you'd discovered about the jewelry and that you were on your way here. If the switch had been an honest mistake, Caldwell would have just called you and explained. I knew there had to be more to it for two people to wind up dead. That got me over here in a hurry. This gate pulled across the hall is a dead giveaway."

"The gate?"

"Fire hazard. These old security gates were outlawed years ago, but not required to be removed. No one would dare use them without risking a huge fine. Somebody was up to something. We found Caldwell and a guy named Russ Landers — he's got a sheet a mile long — upstairs. Damnedest setup I ever saw. They left the display case open, jewels on the floor, set up to look like a robbery had been interrupted before we even got there. The two of them are already being booked at the station. Hauled them right out the front door without their keys," he added as he unlocked the gate and shoved it open.

Sara frowned. "I think Caldwell killed the guard and Chris Wheeler. I've figured it out."

Her brother patted her shoulder. "Be patient. Let me wrap this up, then you can call Bret and explain it to both of us."

"Bret?" *Bret's not upstairs?*

Here? In the building? Steve's eyes widened in alarm.

"Hostage, they took him as a hostage."

Her brother's complexion paled as he straightened up. "There were only two guys up there, Sara. Landers was the one behind you in the passageway."

"What about Riley? Caldwell was talking to Sean Riley on the phone right before he took us hostage! He was on his way over here."

Before Steve could add anything, she spun and raced back down the corridor. Steve caught up with her as they passed Caldwell's office. She pointed up the narrow stairs. Despite the pain in her hip, she took them two at a time again, catching herself at the top, at the very spot where she'd been blindfolded.

Crime scene tape already stretched across the Grand Staircase. Steve pulled out his gun as they dashed across the foyer and into the Greek Room. It was cavernous, bare without patrons and partygoers. Sara wove in and out of the columns, looking behind every statue. Nothing.

With Steve at her heels she went back into the foyer. The storage area. Maybe when the lights had gone out they pushed Bret into the space with her. But the police had gone that way. Think. She yanked Steve with her. She didn't let go until they were in the Egyptian Room.

She raced past the permanent displays, ignoring the case in the middle, not caring if it had been swept clean by Eldridge himself. She looked at the pottery and the cats and the statues until her eye settled on the entrance to the tomb. "He's in there. It's the only place to hide someone."

Steve looked as doubtful as he always did but he followed her. She could tell he was calling and getting no answer but it didn't matter. She motioned for him to follow and stopped in front of the mummy cases. All three cases, which had been open during the fund-raiser, were closed.

"He must be in there," she repeated. "Help me." She tried to open the mummy case. It wouldn't budge. "Push." It took the full force of both of them to finally open the lid. As they pried it open, Bret Sanderson tumbled onto the floor, bound and gagged with duct tape.

From behind the mummy case, Sean Riley sprang forward, yanked Bret up by the shoulder, and waved a revolver at Steve.

"No!" Sara cried.

He pressed the gun to Bret's back and gestured until Steve threw his own gun at Riley's feet and backed across the room.

Fear gripped Sara but she didn't dare turn to watch her brother. "Nobody's going to pin this on me," she thought Riley said. His fair complexion flushed. He looked beyond her and called out something else.

Sara strained to read his lips. Bret was on his knees, his eyes wide and clear.

"No closer." Riley straightened his arm and cocked the revolver.

Sara turned around. Steve nudged her with a roll of duct tape he'd picked up from the floor. Riley yelled. She blinked, straining to understand. Steve made it easy. He looked her in the eye and crossed his wrists against the leg of the display case. "Do as he says," could not have been clearer.

Sara fought her rising panic and the hot tears behind her lids. When she had bound her brother to the case, she threw the tape back at Riley's feet.

"You understand plenty," he said. "Then you'll understand that idiot Caldwell has had

Eldridge in a panic since he told him the real jewels were floating around with two girls." He aimed the gun at Sara then back to Bret. "We knew the minute you realized what you had, the whole scheme would have blown wide open."

"What scheme?" she said as clearly as possible, not caring if she understood his reply or not. It would give her precious seconds to think.

. Again he swung his gun. Perspiration beaded his forehead. "Simple. So simple it went off perfectly when Eldridge did it in Detroit. He put a few of his copies of the jewelry into the exhibit. Then he stole them but left the real stuff thrown around to make it look like a botched robbery. Simple . . ."

Sara touched her throat where she had once worn the necklace. Matt Allen had let them keep everything real, which meant he couldn't have known what his boss was up to. Simple was right. The insurance company would never have known that the stolen items were the fakes.

The barrel of the gun swung to her. Had she said it out loud? The gun trembled slightly in Sean's hand. "I'm not a murderer. Nobody's going to pin Caldwell's crimes on me. Safe passage, that's all I want." He pointed the gun over her shoulder. "Hear me? Safe passage. Caldwell worked it out so he'd be the hero, leave some jewels on the floor as if he had interrupted the thieves. Simple . . ."

Sara watched as he lowered his chin. His mouth went slack as if he were talking to himself. Explain how defrauding an insurance company was worth two lives, she wanted to scream. Explain how money could be worth murder.

Riley yanked Bret to his feet and motioned Sara over.

Without looking at Steve, Sara did as she was commanded. "Use your sign language," he commanded. "Explain that we're leaving. Cooperation is all I want. No funny business. Safe passage. This was none of my doing." Riley hit her elbow. "Tell him!"

Sara signed, *Eldridge planned it; Caldwell screwed it up. Wheeler broke into everything — our apartments, the condos.* Despite the fact that Bret could hear everything, Sara translated frantically, never taking her eyes from Riley's distorted features. *New Year's Eve,* she signed as Riley continued. *Caldwell will tell you I was at that ski place, but it was him. Caldwell drove up there to get the jewelry from Wheeler. Wheeler, the moron, was too scared to tell him he hadn't found anything. Caldwell went into a rage and killed him. He made it look like Wheeler was drunk, passed out in the snow . . . a rage, just like on the roof with the guard the night of the party.*

Sara stood so close she could smell his breath. Desperate, she thought as she tried to keep her own hands calm. *Do what he says,* she added on her own to Bret. *Don't be a hero.*

"You're coming with me," Riley said to both of them. The veins in his neck stood out and his face darkened to crimson as he yelled to Steve.

Sara stumbled forward with Bret still bound and gagged beside her. Her heart pumped furiously as she tried to guess what instructions had been barked at her brother. Steve's service revolver lay at his feet. Riley kicked the gun into the corner as he forced them past Steve and through the Egyptian

Room. The gems and gold, still scattered in the attempt to make the robbery look real, glittered from the floor.

Riley stopped at the Sphinx. He turned full face and pointed at Sara. "Don't move for fifteen minutes. Get back against the wall." He pressed the gun into the middle of Bret's back. "Safe passage. I'll leave him untouched, soon as I'm where I need to go. No funny business and you'll have him back. If I hear you make one move, you'll never see him again."

Sara kept her eyes on Riley as she felt for the nearly invisible knob to the door in the painted panel behind her. Riley's veins still throbbed and his pale blue eyes had faded as if the last of reason had left him. He backed up to the banister cat and forced Bret down the stairs.

Sara spun around. There was no time to free Steve and no reason to trust Riley. Instead she yanked open the door and for the second time, plunged into the storage corridor. It was dim, half lighted. She careened off a stack of chairs as she realized the earlier chase had knocked out bulbs. By now pain was everywhere, pain she'd think about later.

She threw her arms out on either side of her as she limped, then ran, feeling the uneven walls, picking up splinters. When she reached the top of the stairs, she forced herself to stop, forced her breathing into gasps she prayed were silent. She rubbed her hands over her pants and started down the steps. Don't let me be too late, she prayed. Not too late.

She forced one foot in front of the other. In her head she envisioned Riley downstairs pushing, shoving Bret along the main corridor she knew so well. Halfway down the steps she could see light. The door was ajar. Five more steps. Quiet. She took off her sneakers. She stopped and moved by inches, looking into the corridor, in time to glimpse Riley's back as he pushed Bret ahead. They had reached the employees' entrance.

She tore after them and dove at Riley's back. He shoved Bret sideways as she hit Riley full force behind the knees. His arm jerked. The gun flew out of his hand as he crashed headlong through the glass door.

Run, she wanted to cry to Bret as he stood pressed against the wall. Blood trickled down from his hair where a glass shard had nicked him. Run. Instead he leaned to her and pressed his cheek against hers. He didn't move. She swiped at tears as she followed his glance. Riley lay motionless, unconscious in a glittering sea of glass, nearly as bright and shining as the real gems scattered on the floor above her.

She sank against Bret as she pulled the tape off his mouth, then worked on his wrists. The moment he was free his arms were around her, so tight she could feel the pounding of his heart. Together they started back for Steve. For the first time in days there was no need to run.

When Sara Howell's friend Amy is found dead in Shadow Point Park, the police say her death was just an accident. But Sara has seen the rage in Amy's boyfriend Mark. Did he lose control?

Read Hear No Evil #5: SUDDEN DEATH